I0699485

Edited and Proofread by Elaine Richards

https://www.instagram.com/byelliesedits/

Cover Design by Booksnmoods

https://www.booksandmoods.com/

Alpine Ridge Map: Grace Elena and Lizzie A.

For a complete list of content warnings, please check out:

www.graceelenaauthor.com

 Created with Vellum

TENNESSEE ROOTS UNIVERSE

ALPINE RIDGE

MASON POINTE

NASHVILLE

ALPINE RIDGE

BOOK 1.5

A Holiday Novella

CHARACTER CATCH UP

The Tennessee Roots Universe consists of 3 towns: Alpine Ridge, Mason Pointe, and Nashville. Each town has **interconnected standalones** that can be read on their own, but it's recommended to read them in order to prevent any spoilers. It's a big universe, with a variety of characters, I know, but I love it and hope you will too.

If this is your first book of mine, thank you and welcome, I hope you enjoy and find a home here in this universe.

Here are some introductions to characters in this series that were introduced in my debut novel, ***Between the Vines***, and will reappear in this novella.

Camilla Morales and **Bennett Moore** have their own book, *Between the Vines*, which is book one in the Alpine Ridge series. It's grumpy x sunshine, strangers to lovers, the girl next door, and found family. Camilla is the new owner of Stone Vineyard which is where the Christmas party will be held in this novella. Camilla is briefly present in this novella, Bennett is not, but he is mentioned since he is the ex-husband of this novella's FMC, **Katherine Pearson**. Camilla and Bennett have an established relationship in this novella.

Izzy Pearson is Katherine's younger sister and is a side character in both *Between the Vines* and this novella.

Bernadette (Birdy) Lowry is a side character in *Between the Vines* and is best friend's with Camilla. She is a sweets shop owner in the small town. She is only briefly mentioned in this novella.

Steve Robinson is best friend's with Bennett. They are coined Alpine Ridge's golden boys. He is a side character in *Between the Vines* and is dating Birdy toward the end of that novel. He is briefly mentioned in this novella where he is in an established relationship with Birdy.

Peyton Stone used to live in Alpine Ridge until her husband passed. Peyton and her husband used to own Stone Vineyard. She appears briefly in *Between the Vines* with her daughter **Morgan Stone**. Morgan is like a daughter to Bennett and Katherine as they were the ones to take care of her when her father passed while Peyton was overcome with grief. This all happened before *Between the Vines* and is explained in further detail in that novel. Bennett and Camilla end up buying the land in between them to eventually gift to Morgan at the end of their book. Peyton and Morgan appear briefly in this novella.

Lance King appears briefly in *Between the Vines*. He is the MMC in this novella.

Any other characters in this novella that you are unfamiliar with are **new**.

HAPPY READING. <3

To those that felt stuck in their small town, but never left.
You're worth more than the opinion of your past.
It's never too late to change, to be new.
Start now.

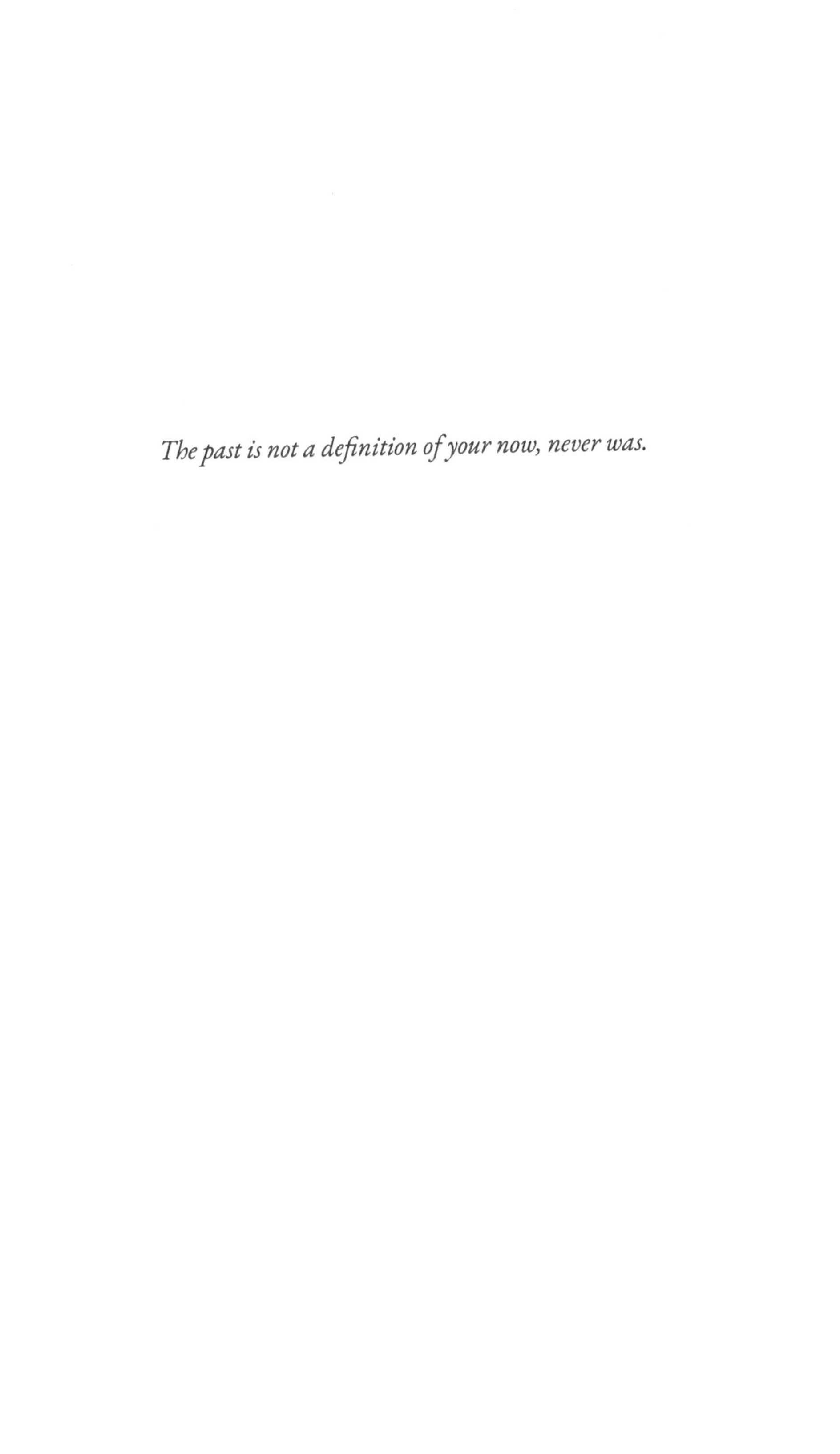

The past is not a definition of your now, never was.

PLAYLIST

people change - Ella Langley
All I Want For Christmas is a Cowboy - Megan Moroney
cowboy like me - Taylor Swift
You're Gonna Go Far - Noah Kahan
Don't Smile - Sabrina Carpenter
Burn, Burn, Burn - Zach Bryan
right where you left me - Taylor Swift
Scared to Start - Michael Marcagi
Used to be Young - Miley Cyrus
Dawns - Zach Bryan, Maggie Rogers
Maroon - Taylor Swift
Happier Than Ever - Billie Eilish
Moving Out - Kacey Musgraves
Am I Okay? - Megan Moroney
Country Never Leaves - Willow Avalon
"Slut!" (Taylor's Version) (From the Vault) - Taylor Swift
The Kind of Love We Make - Luke Combs

Good Graces - Sabrina Carpenter
I would, Would You - Kelsea Ballerini
Man - JoJo
run for the hills - Tate McRae
Stand Still - Sabrina Claudio

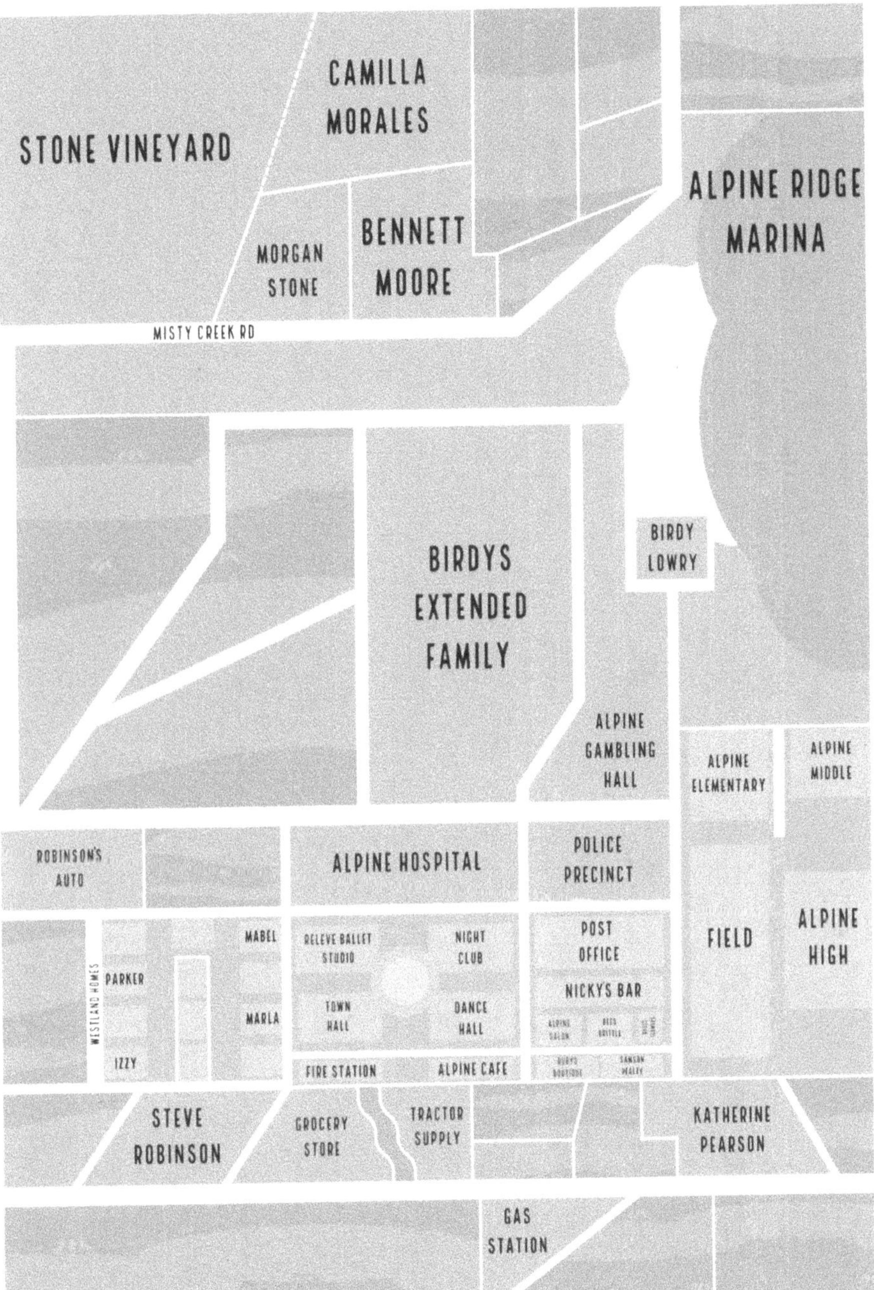
STONE VINEYARD
CAMILLA MORALES
BENNETT MOORE
MORGAN STONE
ALPINE RIDGE MARINA
MISTY CREEK RD
BIRDY LOWRY
BIRDYS EXTENDED FAMILY
ALPINE GAMBLING HALL
ALPINE ELEMENTARY
ALPINE MIDDLE
ROBINSON'S AUTO
ALPINE HOSPITAL
POLICE PRECINCT
FIELD
ALPINE HIGH
WESTLAND HOMES
PARKER
MABEL
MARLA
IZZY
RELEVE BALLET STUDIO
TOWN HALL
NIGHT CLUB
DANCE HALL
POST OFFICE
NICKYS BAR
ALPINE SALON
BETS BRISTLE
BURYS BOUTIQUE
SANSON REALTY
FIRE STATION
ALPINE CAFE
STEVE ROBINSON
GROCERY STORE
TRACTOR SUPPLY
KATHERINE PEARSON
GAS STATION

PROLOGUE

KATHERINE

YOU KNOW what's hard about staying in your hometown after years and years of pain? Sticking it out when it feels like you've outstayed your welcome.

How can it be that I was the one who grew up here, yet I feel like I'm slowly being kicked out of this town?

Alpine Ridge used to be my safe space, my sanctuary. Now, it's become a place where time has stopped for me and continues for everyone else.

It's mostly a pity party though, and it's a party of one. No letters in the mail inviting anyone else. Nope. Just me.

It's been such a strong feeling, a strong pull to get me out of Alpine Ridge and go somewhere new. But where would I go? And do I want to leave everything behind? My family, friends, and memories?

I've never left to explore new places, not even when my sister went on her annual backpacking trips. She even brought Birdy one summer and they fell in love with the mountains.

I'm pretty sure Izzy is returning from her winter trip today from Gatlinburg, and I can't wait to hear all about it. She went with her girlfriend, Haley, whom she met on a solo weekend trip back in July. I met her a few times, but Izzy wanted to keep it under wraps until summer ended. She waited to tell everyone else until September when things started to get serious.

It's sad, really, that I depend on my younger sister to tell me about all her travels, yet I can't even step foot out of this town.

But maybe that changes today.

Or who knows, maybe by Christmas, I'll finally find someone that makes staying in this small town worth a damn.

But not everyone gets a Christmas miracle. And I don't think Santa has me at the top of his list.

ONE

KATHERINE

THE CLASSICAL BALLET music is drifting throughout the studio and it's making me dream of a life as a dancer again with each piano note. It's been years since I've danced in a ballet, but my body still knows exactly what to do.

My feet move where my brain tells them to go, my arms following. My head swivels accordingly and I take deep breaths where needed. I might be getting older, but I feel like I'm eighteen again preparing for a ballet recital. The ones that Alpine Ridge used to host before funding fell through with the program we had in town. Ballet in Alpine Ridge only really resurfaced because I opened up my studio.

I'd be damned if I lost every part of me, including ballet.

It allows me to express myself, pushing my body through all kinds of movements that give me empowerment and discipline. Opening up Relevé allowed for ballet and dance to continue to thrive and show little girls the big dreams they can achieve. It's all I could want, knowing how much it's helped me when I was their age. And, of course, there are the nightly pole and chair dancing classes that help women find their confidence again.

The sound of the bells jingling takes me out of the rehearsed dance and I slip and fall. I wince at the impact and hold my knee which is starting to burn, turning to look at who is coming in at this time. I thought I put the closed sign up, but I guess I forgot.

It's Camilla Morales.

She's wearing a puffy white jacket with some black leggings and winter boots. Pretty positive all of this winter gear is from Chicago, her hometown.

"So sorry, Kat! I couldn't hear the music until I opened the door. Didn't mean to mess up your routine."

She walks further into the studio, and I get up, dusting off my hands.

"It's fine, I was just going through an old one. Nothing too important."

Camilla's brown eyes glisten before she tunes into the music still playing. "Is this The Nutcracker?"

I nod, heading to my phone that's on the table nearby. It's connected wirelessly to the speakers installed into the ceiling, a cool feature I added a year ago so I didn't have to haul around a big speaker.

"It's Christmastime, so I figured I'd get started with the music."

"Do you plan to decorate the studio, too?" she asks behind me. I turn to see her admiring the studio.

God, I remember months ago meeting her. It honestly feels like years. She fit so perfectly into this town that I couldn't bear to hate her. There's no reason to; she walks into every room holding enough sunshine for herself and others.

Bennett picked a good one.

"Not yet, I think this weekend. Have you decorated your place or the vineyard?" I ask, pressing pause on the playlist.

She nods. "Yeah, Bennett and Birdy have been taking over the vineyard while I decorate my place. I heard you guys try to map out people's decorated homes so the residents can do a drive-by of some sort?"

"Yeah, it's a cute thing we try to do for each other. Last year,

Birdy had a huge inflatable Grinch on her lawn and the kids loved it."

"I can't wait to see how everyone decorates, then!" She beams.

"So what brings you by?" I ask, clearing my throat. I don't mean to be rude, but I was hoping to practice this dance all night. Call it self-care, or whatever.

Camilla's eyes widen and her cheeks redden. "Oh! Duh, so sorry. The party next weekend..."

"At the vineyard? I heard bits about it," I reply. Marla, a boutique owner, was talking about it when I was dress shopping a few days ago and I was *definitely* eavesdropping. I assumed it was just a casual party where anyone could go, but I guess not with the looks of Camilla coming to me in person. Was she here to invite me?

"Yeah, it's going to be really sweet. Birdy wanted me to stop by and give you a formal invite since she's super busy event planning and decorating." Camilla pulls an envelope out of her winter coat pocket and hands it to me. I open it, and it's a beautiful red card with gold lettering.

"Oh," slips out of my mouth.

A Christmas party invitation, and Camilla's vineyard address.

"Thanks," I say with a smile. She nods before pushing hair behind her ear nervously.

"I hope you can make it. I know Morgan would love to see you."

"She's coming to town?" I haven't had time to reach out to Peyton about Morgan this week, so I'm glad I can get some kind of information about them, regardless if it's from my ex-husband's girlfriend.

"Yep, Peyton, too. Obviously." She giggles nervously.

"I'll be there. I'll call Peyton too to see if they want to stay with me," I say.

Camilla's eyes widen again and my heart drops.

"She's staying with Bennett. Sorry, I thought you knew."

I chew on the inside of my cheek for a moment, attempting to not let my emotions get the best of me.

You're not left behind. You're not left behind. You're not—

"Of course, silly me." I dismiss my thoughts with a wave of my hand. "They've been doing that since the divorce. It's nothing new. I don't know why I even mentioned it."

Camilla is quiet as she takes in my words. She takes a step closer, and it's like I can feel her trying to emanate warmth...and a hug. I'm not sure if a hug from her would cure any of my feelings right now. It might do the opposite.

"You'll always be her favorite, you know."

My heart stops for a slight second, and I'm not sure if it's from all of the dancing or because of my racing thoughts, but my body breaks out in a sweat. My hands form into fists before relaxing them. "I know. Thanks for the invite, Camilla. I'll make sure to be there." It's a promise.

She smiles before backing up and heading toward the door. "I can't wait to celebrate Christmas with you. We're still on for that dance lesson next week?"

Right, I've been teaching Camilla a few dance routines just for fun. Birdy pops in sometimes and even drags Izzy. It's like a small girl's night here, and it sometimes makes me want to stay in this town forever.

It makes me feel like I belong once more.

"Yeah, we're good to go for that."

Camilla waves before leaving the studio and I stand there, fingers intertwined, picking at the skin of my cuticles.

Christmas in Alpine Ridge will be a good one this year. I'm just not sure if it will be my last.

TWO

LANCE

IT'S hard growing out of the mold your small town puts you in.

Lance the player. Lance the playboy. Lance the jock turned drunk. Lance the arrogant.

Lance. Lance. Lance.

I got so tired of the small town gossip that I decided to just fucking own the titles. Who cares, right? Might as well just let them see who they made me.

I'm not a drunk, though, never was. *That* is one title I won't let them make of me. Having a father as a drunk was something I had no choice in. But, alas, he's six feet under and it's better that way. *I'm* better that way.

But since there's a damn assumption about me drinking too much, I just tend to hangout at the bar on the outskirts of town so I don't have to bump into anyone I know. There are some older locals, but it's usually some folks from Mason Pointe who are trying to hide from their town, too.

Like a small town bar full of misfits and unwanted folks, we don't judge here and we certainly don't pry into each other's lives. We just order our drinks and go about our night.

It's the perfect hideaway and I guess it fits with the name of the dive bar:

The Lost Cowboy

We're all just lost men trying to find a place in this world, succumbing to the vice of cheap beer and darts.

"Another, Lance?" the bartender asks, reaching for my glass. I nod and hand it to her as I adjust the ball cap on my head.

Lainey Tills is a sweet girl, but she's got to get out of this town. She's got big dreams to be a country star in Nashville and is working this job to save enough for a place there. I make sure to tip her extra whenever she serves me.

There are weekend nights where we have some singers go up on stage for an hour or two and Lainey has done it a couple of times. That's how I know she's fucking good at what she does. She sings from the soul and her original songs are better than the covers she occasionally belts.

She hands me a full glass before getting another patron. I immediately start drinking the ice cold beer before heading back to the darts area where I met a few guys earlier. They're tossing darts and laughing as I walk up.

They're deep in conversation about their weekend plans of getting last minute Christmas gifts and going to the square to get Christmas trees. It's Friday night and Christmas is next weekend, so everyone is hustling to get things done in time.

"What about you, Lance?" one of the guys, Tanner, asks. I give them a look before laughing and Tanner's brows pinch in confusion.

"I don't really celebrate Christmas."

"Really?" another, I think his name is Derrick, asks. The third drinks his beer. I'm gonna be honest, I have no fucking idea what his name is. He's wearing a Carhartt jacket, so I've just called him that in my head.

I shrug. "I go to my mom's for dinner, if that counts. But I don't decorate my place or go out of my way to go to events."

"Kinda like Scrooge."

The comment stings like an insult and I feel like I need to get out of there. We've been playing darts for an hour already and this is my third beer from Lainey. I could do an Irish exit, but that's not my forte, despite my reputation of being a dick around this town. Plus, I got a tab to close out.

"I'll own it," I joke. The guys all look at me, and Carhartt is still drinking his beer.

I hold back from rolling my eyes. They're probably from Mason Pointe. Some are cool, but the majority that I meet from that town are pricks. Worse than the titles I've been given around here. They're living proof of them.

"One more round?" Tanner cuts in, pointing to the darts board with his beer cup. The other guys nod and grunt in agreement before they start a new game. It's like they're in their own world again without me. I don't bother telling them that I want in. Because I don't.

I chug the remaining beer and book it to the bar to pay my tab. Lainey sees the look on my face and doesn't bother asking, and before I know it, my card and receipt are on the counter.

"Thanks, Lain," I say while signing and giving her a hefty tip.

She puckers her lips. "Not staying late tonight?"

I shake my head. "Gotta get to bed, you know grandpas and their bedtimes."

She laughs, her blue eyes brightening under the neon signs above. "Sure. You're so old, Lance. Just get home safely, please."

"Always do," I tell her confidently. I hear some whoops and hollers near the front door, and Lainey laughs.

"It's working!"

I almost ask her what she's talking about, but she's already moving to get someone's drink order.

I head to the entrance where a group of six is coming in. There's a couple kissing and I roll my eyes and huff out a breath. They get out of my way just in time when I'm nearing the door-frame. The draft from outside is cold and I silently curse myself for not bringing a jacket. December in Tennessee isn't *that* cold, so I wore a long sleeve. We're not expecting snow until January.

Before I can make it out of the bar, I bump into someone and she makes a yelping sound. The flash of red instantly blinds me and I grab her shoulders to steady her.

"Sorry, Darlin'," I say almost immediately. She lifts her head and there's whooping and hollering behind us.

What the hell is going on at this hour? Are people going insane tonight?

"Fuck, sorry, wasn't watching where I was going—" When she finally looks up, her green eyes catch mine and it's like the world stops.

Katherine Pearson.

This is the last place I'd expect Miss Pearson to end up. Is this a dream? Am I truly so drunk that I'm imagining all of this?

"Lance?" she asks loudly, breaking me out of my thoughts. I drop my hands from her shoulders.

"Kiss already!" Someone yells behind us. I pinch my brows, wondering what the hell they're saying that for.

"Fuck, she didn't." Katherine sighs. She's looking up and I follow her gaze.

A damn mistletoe is hanging above the bar door. I hear a laugh and it's—

"Lainey," Katherine and I both say at the same time.

THREE

KATHERINE

I CAME to *The Lost Cowboy* to clear my head and here I am, under a damn mistletoe with the last man I'd expect to be here.

Lance King.

I haven't seen him around town the last few months, and honestly, I thought that he packed his bags and left. A part of me wanted to go with him, if that were the case.

There's more hollering in the bar and it's making me feel anxious. My hands clench into fists and I need a shot or three.

Lance's blue eyes are boring into mine and his jaw ticks. His eyes are swarming with thoughts that I can't read. Does he want to...?

"It'll shut them up," he says, finally breaking the silence.

I glance quickly at the bar where Lainey is waving liquor bottles in her hands before clinking them. I shake my head at her.

"No? Of course, sorry for even saying that," Lance continues.

"What?" I say, turning back to him. Oh, he thought I was shaking my head at *him*.

"Hurry up before you owe us all shots!" someone yells. That's when Lance and I look at the wall next to us and there's a sign that looks brand new.

No mistletoe kiss, drinks are on you

"Fuck, let's get this over with." I finally concede.

Lance nods before twisting his ball cap so it's backward. I'm watching him in slow motion and it's mesmerizing for some reason. I've never really paid any mind to Lance King, but *now I am*.

I get on my tiptoes to reach up, my hand going to his shoulder. One of his hands goes to my hip and another under my chin. I close my eyes, hoping he doesn't hear my racing heart.

"I'm gonna kill Lainey." He breathes before I feel his lips on mine. I stiffen at how soft they are. We continue to kiss and there's noise behind us, but I drown it all out. His grip tightens on my hip and his thumb caresses my cheek for a moment.

There's tightness in my stomach and I'm not sure if I'm nauseous or it's butterflies.

Or both.

We finally pull back and it's like the world has been put back on *play* because no one is focusing on us anymore. Except Lainey. She's still screaming like a maniac.

If she thinks this mistletoe idea will go very far, I've got news for her.

"I'll see you," Lance quickly says before adjusting his hat back to normal. I open my mouth to say something, but I'm still in shock.

I lift my fingers to my lips before I see him walk out of the bar and continue to the parking lot. His white truck is like a beacon in the night and I watch him for a good moment as he gets in, pulls out, then drives off.

There are more people piling into the bar and I move to make room for them, still mentally frozen from what just happened.

I kissed Lance King. I honestly can't remember the last time I kissed someone like this.

And I enjoyed it. Which scares the living shit out of me to admit.

LAINEY IS CLOSING out all the tabs before she's pushing a water in my direction. I thank her before sipping it. It's around two in the morning, and I barely left this seat except to go change the music at the jukebox in the corner.

Almost everyone's gone and I feel like an old man just waiting to be kicked out for outstaying my welcome.

"You're moping and I need you to chug that," Lainey states from the other side of the bar, a rag in her hand ready to start on closing work.

I look at her for a moment before nodding and chugging. The water is much needed, I can already feel the hangover that's brewing for tomorrow. Thankfully, I don't have any lessons until the afternoon.

"Not moping, by the way," I tell her. She laughs before wiping the counter and making her way to me. The other workers are cleaning tables, flipping chairs, and making a ruckus behind me. Despite the noise, it's like Lainey and I are in a bubble right now and she's all that I'm focused on.

"Keep telling yourself that."

"What?" I sigh.

She purses her lips before leaning over the counter. She grabs my free hand and holds it tightly, I let her. "Something is going on and I'm here if you need to talk about it."

My throat feels tight all of a sudden and I hate it. "This is very disturbing to realize."

Her bright blue eyes are locked on mine. "Disturbing? How so?"

I nod toward the bar behind her, and then look up at the ceiling. "That I'm finding solace with my bartender. I should be in therapy, not here."

She laughs before releasing my hand and grabbing my empty glass before refilling it. I thank her before drinking it.

"I'm not just your bartender, Katherine. I'd like to think we're acquaintances. Maybe one day...friends?"

Friends.

Growing up in a small town and dating Bennett toward the end of my high school years made it hard to keep female friendships. We were so madly in love that we forgot about everyone; we were in a Katherine and Bennett bubble that it felt like I lost touch with so many people unintentionally. We were too young—at an age where it felt like it was all or nothing when we found each other. Then the isolation period of when he left for his deployments didn't help. I was a scared little 20 something year old who didn't know how to really make friends.

I get jealous, I will admit, seeing girl groups walking around town. Birdy and Camilla have of course invited me to many hangouts the last few months, but it felt mandatory. Or at least it did for me.

I'm not sure if I'm *capable* of making new friends at this age. Thirty-seven years old and I'm here contemplating the woes of life with a bartender. *Wow.*

"Do you think that's possible?" I ask, honestly. A hiccup follows and I cover my mouth quickly. Lainey smiles and a laugh slips out of my lips. "Sorry."

"No need to apologize. Don't ever apologize for something you didn't do wrong." I look at her for a moment, and she continues. "I think it's very feasible. You're never too far in life to *not* make new friends. We can go easy, too."

"Easy?" I almost laugh, but her face is serious.

"Come to my show tomorrow night. It's an hour set, but I promise that I'll make it worth it for my new friend."

The Lost Cowboy does live shows every Friday and Saturday night, at least that's what I read on their huge marquee out front when I arrived. I missed today since I came so late...and then the whole mistletoe mishap happened with Lance.

The man that I haven't seemed to get out of my mind the last few hours. It's like he's infiltrated my thoughts, and it's new to me. Very new to me.

"Deal. But please don't sing *Wagon Wheel*. It's way overplayed," I say.

She smiles and shakes her head. "I was thinking more of Dolly Parton or Megan Moroney."

"And an original, I hope?"

She grabs the rag that she abandoned and nods before she starts to clean again. "A few, I think, are ready to be heard. I'm a little nervous, though, so I'll see if I want to sing them all."

I've yet to hear her sing, so I can't say any encouraging words at this moment. I just nod and smile, hoping that's sufficient.

"Can't wait. Do you need me to bring flowers or something? Tell you to break a leg?"

"God, no!" Lainey laughs. "Just show up and try not to kiss that same cowboy under the mistletoe...or do. Y'all were cute, I can't lie."

My cheeks burn and I cover them up with my hands. God, this is embarrassing. I need to go home right now.

"Lance is just someone I know."

Lainey looks at me like I just told her pigs fly. She knows I'm lying. Damn, maybe she will be a good friend to have in my life. Call me out on my bullshit.

"Sure, he is. Maybe he'll just happen to be here again. He thinks I'll make it big in Nashville one day."

This piqued my interest. She knows him?

"Oh, really?"

Her eyes sparkle and she nods. "That's my big dream, Katherine. I want all of it. The glitz, the glamor, and the sold-out arenas. It'll take some years of performing, but I know deep in my soul it's for me."

Her enthusiasm—and optimism—is contagious and gets me thinking about my own life. Do I have this kind of dream like she does?

I've always wanted to open up a ballet studio and here I am owning a very successful one. But is there more for me?

"I'll be there tomorrow. And I'm going to order an Uber," I tell her, getting up so I'm not holding up the staff from closing. I drove here, but driving after a few drinks is the last thing I need to worry about. I can just grab my car in the morning.

She holds up a finger for me to wait, runs to the end of the bar, and returns with an ice-cold water bottle.

I thank her before waving goodbye and pulling my phone out to call an Uber as I head outside. The cold December air bites my skin, but I like how it feels. It makes me feel alive and I look up at the dark sky.

Alpine Ridge has the prettiest skies at night. So many stars to count and dream on. I close my eyes and for a moment, I think of a wish.

I make it.

My phone pings and I open my eyes, looking down. My Uber is arriving soon.

Let's just hope my wish will too.

FOUR
LANCE

I'M NOT sure why I can't stop thinking about Katherine Pearson, but here I am in broad daylight, thinking of the woman I kissed last night.

The memory of her soft lips against mine makes my body react in a way that it hasn't in a while. And it kind of terrifies me.

I haven't slept with someone in a hot minute and that's new for me and my *playboy* reputation. I simply had better things to focus on last summer than to chase women.

While out at the stables tending to the horses, my phone buzzes from my back pocket.

This ranch was my dad's before he passed, and while I'd like to say it's one of the best in Alpine Ridge, it's not even on the map. It's not a place people willingly go to or know about.

It's just a rundown place that had potential before my dad's alcoholism took over in his late twenties. My mom tried to take care of it, but overcome with grief, she's been holed up in the cottage up the hill about a mile away. So in turn, I care for the ranch just for her.

LAINEY

Hey stud

I chuckle before thinking of a response. I honestly forgot that Lainey and I exchanged numbers. As pretty and talented as she is, I see her as more of a sibling than anything. Or even a best friend. And those are some that I rarely have.

ME

What's up superstar

LAINEY

Coming over tonight?

She's talking about the live music tonight at *The Lost Cowboy*.

I fire back a response while I mix the feed for the five horses. It's a tedious task with how old the horses are, but I cherish them. One of the horses, Hershey, was from when I turned eighteen and my mom found him getting ready for the slaughterhouse auction a few towns over.

He was in pretty bad shape, so my mom begged my dad to bring him home. My dad could never say no to her, but he couldn't ever say no to the liquor so I'm not sure how much that truth holds up.

He coined the cute name not just because of his rich brown coat, but when he initially came to the stables, it was past Halloween, and he found a bag full of Hershey's in the stall that my parents would end up putting him in. Since he was so emaciated from his previous owners, he took one good look at the bag of my hidden stash and swallowed it whole; bag and all. It was quite an expensive vet visit, but he made it through and he's been living his best life since.

ME

Of course. Can't wait to tell you to break a leg.

LAINEY

fuck you!!

ME

I laugh before putting my phone away and grabbing as many pails as I can, heading to each horse's stable. Majority of them are munching on hay as I make my way into their area and drop off the feed, but when I get to Hershey's, he's looking at me with his sad old man eyes.

There isn't much time left for him on Earth, so I try to make it the best it can be. I don't ride him anymore and I let him live out on the pasture for as long as he can take it. He's a spoiled horse too, getting all the blankets during the winter time.

He's also one of the horses that I don't need to use a halter and lead rope. He's so well behaved and timid that he walks wherever I go and answers when I call for him. And right now, he's eying the pail of feed.

"You're starving, huh?" I joke as I push my way into his stall and rub his muzzle. He leans into my touch while I put his pail down. I take my time in his stall, longer than the other ones, just touching him and running my hands through his mane.

He's a beautiful quarter horse that apparently won many races in his younger days until he was used so much that his legs gave out one race.

It showed me the true heart of my mother when she finally got the courage to tell me Hershey's story. She couldn't bear to tell me the moment she gifted me him, but it was when I was around twenty years old when she sat me down after I noticed Hershey limping one day out on the pasture.

She's the reason why I stay in Alpine Ridge, to be honest. A good woman who loved her husband even when he chose the bottle over her most days. She loved me until she knew I was able to love myself, and because of that, I'll never leave this town if she's still in it.

As much as I have those days where I feel like I no longer belong in Alpine Ridge, she keeps me planted here. My roots are in this small town.

Hershey neighs and brings me out of my thoughts, so I smooth my palm over his body once more before he rubs his head against my shoulder and then chest. He's my baby, as big as he is; I'd do anything for this old man.

"Eat, you need it. I added some carrots to the mix," I tell him softly while patting his cheek. He huffs before motioning his head as if he's nodding. He leans down and starts munching on the feed that will give him all the nutrients that hay doesn't.

As I make my way out of the stables, I look up at the sky and see the sunrise starting to rise even further up bringing the most beautiful glow against the hills and faint mountains. I've never been up to the Smoky Mountains, despite being so close. Just never had a reason to.

I add that to a mental bucket list of places to go to, even if it's for a weekend getaway, but with who? I'm not sure.

That's when the silliest idea sprouts into my mind, into the crevices of my well-shelled and protected heart.

The idea of getting to know the girl I've known my whole life, yet I barely know a thing about her. Getting to know her so well that she helps me scratch off a few things from my bucket list.

It warms my heart in a way I haven't felt in a while. And I really like it.

I continue to look at the sunrise, imagining a world where I truly do stay in Alpine Ridge and don't run away just because things might get hard.

MOM'S HOUSE is quiet as I shuffle inside, kicking off my boots and placing them perfectly next to her shoes near the door. There's a faint glow down the hallway—she doesn't like to keep tons of lights on, yet even when it's as bright as it is today, she likes to keep the majority of the curtains closed.

"Ma? You in the living room?" I ask, heading down the hall.

She's sitting with needles and a ball of yarn, knitting her next big project. Presumably, Christmas presents for the grandkids.

My brother, Knox King, lives in Colorado with his wife who he met in college. He's five years older than me and got out of this town as soon as he could. I was surprised he didn't try to leave when he was in high school.

He's got three beautiful children that I see every other Christmas. Since his wife, Stella, is from Florida, they try to go see her family there as well.

"I think Oppy will like this sweater," Ma says, holding up the small bunch of knitted yarn. I can't see the pattern yet, but I trust her. She's got a knack for knitting and everything she touches turns to gold. She mentioned wanting to also crochet some things, but I guess she chose knitting this go around.

I have a whole drawer full of socks and sweaters that she's made for me. Even an ugly Christmas sweater where there's a reindeer holding Santa bridal style. It's goofy and I still have no idea how the hell she knitted that, let alone got the idea for it. It's become a crowd favorite though anytime I wear it out in public.

"She loves everything you make," I agree, sitting down on the loveseat across from her.

She puts her needles down on her lap and looks up. Her black hair is up in a bun, but I can see some of the gray hairs peeking through. She's probably got an appointment at the salon soon, that's one of the things she refuses to give up. Says she feels younger when she gets her hair done. Dad used to take her to the appointments until he couldn't physically. Bed ridden from a bad liver will do that to ya.

"I might make some winter hats this time for the boys." She nods, looking out the massive window that has its curtains drawn. I get up quickly to open it up and the light immediately soaks the room in warmth. The front yard has some lights around the trees for the holiday. There are some decorations as well on the porch that I helped pick out a few weeks ago, though I have yet to put them up for her. I make a quick mental note to do it before Christmas arrives.

"They'll love it," I tell her, finally. She's still staring outside when I settle back down on the loveseat.

"Hershey still doing good?"

I nod. "He's getting older, but acts like a foal sometimes. Still likes to push his head against my chest like he used to all those years ago."

This brings a smile to her face. Hershey was undeniably her favorite of the bunch. Even out of the ones they've rescued before Hershey, so that's saying a lot.

"Good. That's good," she says softly. "I got a call from Poppy Lowry."

Birdy's mom. That's odd. "What did she want?" I ask, irritated.

"Oh, calm down, Lance. She just wanted to ask if I was going to the big Christmas party at Stone Vineyard next Saturday."

"And are you?"

She nods. "Told her that you'd be there too. Asked why Birdy hasn't reached out to you yet about it."

I shrug. "Birdy and I are acquaintances to say the least." Memories of this past summer surface. The fair, and how I was clearly too in my head, trying to flirt with a woman who didn't want anything to do with me.

There have been times where I wanted to call her up to apologize for how I acted this summer, but never did. She's with Steve now, so it doesn't matter anymore.

Bennett comes to mind and then Katherine, of course. They've been divorced for years, but it still feels odd not thinking of them as a pair.

It feels almost wrong thinking of the fact that I kissed Katherine last night. There's a part of me that thinks Bennett will show up any second now to clock me in the jaw for kissing his wife. But he's with Camilla now, and as far as I can tell, they're the happiest couple here in Alpine Ridge.

Just another sad realization that people around me are moving on and I'm at a standstill. People are moving on, meeting new people, and making a new life with them. Even though they're still rooted in this town, they're making new memories.

I want that too.

"Well," Ma starts, "I hope you're able to make it. What plans do you have today?"

I think about my day. I usually tend to the ranch before working on other ranches or farms nearby. That's my main job, at least—to make a living. With all my knowledge of ranching and tending to animals in all sizes, I'm able to help out either newer ranches or help long term ones. It pays really good money and it doesn't feel like work.

But at the end of the day, it feels great to come home and tend to Hershey. I had to be honest with myself a long time ago that at this point, Hershey and I are a pair. We're basically emotional support for each other.

Who the hell thought I'd have an emotional support horse? Not me, but here we are.

"I'll be helping out the Jensens to tame a new horse. Reminds me a lot like Hershey and where he came from."

Ma looks at me and a big smile comes to her face. "You're a good man, Lance. I'm proud of how far you've come."

This makes me emotional, as much as I hate to admit it. My throat tightens and I try to blink away the mist that starts to form in my eyes.

"Thanks, Ma. That means a lot."

She hums in response before continuing on with her sweater. It's quiet as we sit in the living room, basking in the warm sun that's pouring through the windows. She continues to knit and I focus on the sounds of the metal needles clicking against one another.

FIVE

KATHERINE

MY ANKLE IS BURNING after falling during my routine. The girls in the class rush to the small kitchen in the back to grab a bag of ice, which was the nicest thing.

"Are you going to be okay, Miss Kat?" one of the girls, Frances, asks.

I nod, wincing, when I try to readjust to a sitting position on the floor. They offer to stuff their winter coats behind my back on the wall, but I decline.

"I'll be fine, promise. Just a sprain. I think I went a little too hard on that last turn."

There are five girls in this class who primarily take ballet. I do some dance choreography classes as well, but that's not my personal favorite. I try to help the girls around town as much as I can with whatever dance passion they may have. But I favor—as much as I hate to admit it—the ballet girls the most.

They all look at me with big puppy eyes as if I just broke my ankle. It's just a simple sprain that I need to ice and rest, and then I'll be good to go. This happens way more often now that I'm older.

"Don't take your age for granted, girls," I joke as I nod for them to get up from the ground. They start to circle around me like vultures. I need them to still get their routine down for the Christmas dance recital next Friday night.

Jordan, one of the younger girls, has been forgetting a lot of the footwork that I wanted her to practice more of today. She stands up and goes to her place, ready to continue. I can't help but give her a proud smile as the other girls nod and get up as well, following her lead.

"Alright, girls," I shout from the floor, "from the top... Five, six, seven, eight."

They start their routine once more and it's almost flawless, until Jordan mixes up one of the spins and falls down. The other girls run to her to help her up.

"Thanks," she says quietly, looking at me for a moment. It's the look of *oh, shit I messed up please don't yell at me.*

"All good," I reassure them all, making sure I make eye contact with Jordan for a second longer. I clap my hands before pressing the ice pack to my ankle. "One more time, and then we can take a longer break."

They all nod and start the routine once more. This time they're having more fun with it, there are more smiles all around. This is why I love to teach—the passion that you can see in their bodies and faces when they're in the middle of the routine.

It reminds me of when I was younger and just starting out in ballet. I had so much fun, even when I tripped or fell during practice.

Thirty minutes later, the girls are all gone and I'm cleaning up the studio when the door chimes. I turn to see my sister walking in with a red scarf around her neck and a big puffy white sweater.

"Is it that cold out already?" I ask, putting my cleaning supplies away and heading to her. She's all smiles as we side hug.

"Kinda, honestly. I think we're going to have a harsh winter this year."

I raise a brow. "That's unusual for Tennessee, especially here."

"I know. Maybe we'll finally have a white Christmas. Anyway,

I'm here because we need to go out. I had the worst shift. Horrible tips. I need a drink far away from here."

Izzy is pouting and giving me a look just like my girls did earlier today. Except this time, I can't say no to my baby sister. "Sure, where do you wanna go?"

Her eyes brighten for a moment before she wiggles her brows. "What about *The Lost Cowboy*?"

I roll my eyes. "Seriously? I was just there last night. A little too late, I might add." I didn't tell her that I already promised Lainey I'd be there tonight, but that would cause a series of questions that I wasn't ready for.

"What for? Lainey wasn't singing."

"No reason," I tell her, and it isn't a lie. I just randomly showed up there, needing to get out of Alpine without leaving the town line. I would've gone to Mason Pointe, but I chose not to.

It was nice talking to Lainey, and the thought of her asking if we could be friends one day comes to the forefront of my mind.

I do want that, but I'm scared. And that's the most honest I've been with myself lately. Admitting fear isn't something I really like to do–I sidestep until I'm forced to confess. My marriage with Bennett was a perfect example of that–I danced around big decisions and my feelings until he had to make a decision for us that I was too scared to make first.

Maybe I need to stop doing that and just admit my fears and face them head on.

"Well, if you want to grab a drink with me and support Lainey from the front row, come. We can even play darts or billiards."

"You sure you don't want to go shopping or hiking?" I ask, offering other places that aren't another dive bar that she just ended her shift at. *Nicky's* is more for us locals, though, so I get her wanting a change in scenery—even if it's a similar environment.

She deadpans before laughing. "Since when do we hike?"

I smile. "I know, it was worth a try. We can go, but you're driving. Or paying for Uber."

She nods. "Deal. Are you heading home now? I can come with. Think I got a few outfits still in your guest closet."

"You mean your room?" I laugh. Izzy spends half her time at my place or her girlfriends. I'm still not sure why she even has a townhome when she is clearly never there.

"*Guest* room," she reiterates. "You done here?"

I grab the keys to close up and nod. "Yep, all done. Did you drive to work today or do you need a ride to my place?"

"Haley dropped me off," she says as we start to walk out of the studio and I lock up. Today I don't have night classes, which I'm thankful for.

"Perfect. You're paying for dinner, I haven't eaten much today," I tell her as we head to my car. She skips a little as we walk and it's cute. She does it when she's happy.

"Deal!" she sing-songs.

THE LOST COWBOY is busy tonight.

Izzy grabs my elbow and pulls me toward the bar, having to squeeze in between many bodies. I don't think I've ever seen it this busy, but I also haven't really been a regular here until now.

That's embarrassing, I think to myself. Becoming a regular at a *dive bar*. God, I should really start therapy soon instead of finding solace in a place like here.

"Lainey is getting ready, look!" Izzy says, pointing to the stage. I turn to look at her as she's plugging in her guitar and fluffing up her big, blonde hair. If I could explain her stage presence, it would be Dolly Parton mixed with Taylor Swift. Her confidence is off the charts—I can feel it from here and she hasn't even started her set.

"Let's get some drinks, and then we can head to the front of the stage," I suggest. Izzy nods before we finally reach the counter and orders a round of tequila shots to get started as well as some cranberry vodkas to hold us down while we're up near the stage. She hands her card to the bartender as they get pushed in front of us.

There's a chuckle beside me, and I can somehow sense exactly who it might be. I turn and see none other than Lance fucking King. Izzy is too busy signing her receipt when I give him a look.

"No mistletoe around us, so don't even think about it," I say loudly. His eyes sparkle and a smirk surfaces.

"Wasn't even thinking that," he says, leaning in closer to my ear. It gives me chills and I swear there are goosebumps rising all over my body. And there's something in my stomach. Butterflies?

What the hell is happening to me?

I grab my tequila shot and turn to look at Izzy before nodding. She squeals as we clink shot glasses. We take the shot and then bite into the limes that the bartender offered us. Lance watches the whole thing with the biggest grin. If I could read his mind, I'd think he'd be saying something smart, or honestly something about being proud of us. And the latter makes more butterflies swarm my stomach.

"God, that was awful." Izzy gags for a moment before slamming her shot glass down. The bartender comes back with our mixed drinks in cheap plastic cups. We thank him before I turn to Lance once more.

"You're stalking me, Cowboy."

With a beer in his hand, he points toward his chest. "Me? As much as it pains me to admit, I've become a regular here. I haven't seen *you* here until last night."

I narrowed my eyes on him. "Fine, you're not a stalker. Are you here with some boys or alone?" I don't mean my last few words to come out with a tone, but they do. I bite my lip, and he looks at me for a moment before smirking again.

"Not alone, I'm here for someone."

"Yeah? Who's the lucky girl?" He looks past me and nods. I

follow his gaze to the stage and then whip my head around to give him a stunned look. "Huh?"

"Lainey," he states plainly.

I'm not sure what the hell is happening, but there's a twinge of…jealousy that's coursing through me with the way he says her name. He's not even saying it in an endearing or *we're dating* way. Because first of all, if they *are* dating, I'll knock him in the jaw right now for kissing me in front of her last night.

"Really?" I manage to squeak out.

His bright blue eyes watch me for a second before another damn smirk fills his face. I'm about to fucking slap it off him if he continues.

"Yes, really. She's become one of my many good friends. Just wanna see her play tonight. Talent like this is rare and she deserves all eyes on her."

"I heard," I tell him with a bite to my words. His eyes narrow this time, and he's either trying to think of something clever to say back or I've made Lance King speechless.

He takes a deep breath. "She's just a friend."

There's a moment of silence between us two. I've completely forgotten about my sister for a moment, really sucked into this conversation with Lance. Is he trying to convince me that they're amicable? I really shouldn't care. I *really* shouldn't.

"Okay," is all I respond before taking a sip of my mixed drink. There's a nudge at my back and I turn to see my sister finally getting my attention.

"She's about to start, so either finish this convo with Lance and come up with me to the stage, or stay here!"

I think for a moment how much I want to stay with Lance, but I shouldn't. I look back at him and his eyes are expectant. For what? I'm not sure. I give him a smile before nodding toward the stage.

"See you after her set?"

He lifts his beer and I push my plastic cup against it. "See you, Katherine."

The name spills out of his lips like honey and it makes those damn butterflies perform like they're in a circus.

Even when I move toward the stage with my sister, I still feel his gaze on me. I turn back a few times throughout the set and meet his eyes every time.

Fuck.

SIX

LANCE

LAINEY APPROACHES our table with a tray full of shots. "Thank you so much for coming to see me play! I was so nervous, but I hope I did well?"

Izzy, Katherine, and I all nod, Izzy even claps for a moment. Katherine laughs and stands up to hug Lainey.

"You did amazing, you really do have the talent for Nashville," Katherine says loudly. Lainey beams and blushes before sitting down. We all take the shots, as much as I hate them. I'll sip through a cold beer or mixed drink, but shots for some reason are my least favorite. Not sure if it's because it reminds me of my dad, or just a preference.

Katherine is next to me and her arm presses against mine for a moment as she leans forward. She's facing Izzy and resuming her conversation about some kind of dance recital that's happening next weekend.

"Hey," Lainey says, heading to the chair next to me. I pull it out for her and she takes a seat. "You didn't tell me to break a leg."

I shrug. "Figured my text was enough. You did great, by the way."

Her eyes brighten. "Thanks, Lance. Y'all come together?

Didn't get a chance to see you walk in tonight," she says, nodding toward Katherine. She's still deep in conversation with Izzy, so I don't think they're paying any attention to either of us.

I shake my head. "No, we just happened to show up at the same time."

Lainey looks at me, as if she's wanting to ask a million questions. I can see it in her eyes. She wants to know more. She's playing damn matchmaker.

All because of that fucking mistletoe.

I lean back in my chair and she continues to stare. "What?" I ask.

"I might actually do it," she finally says. I cross my arms over my chest and raise a brow.

"Do what?"

She rolls her eyes. "You know, leave Alpine."

It's like I've been struck by lightning and I sit up. "Now?"

"No, silly," she laughs, pushing some strands of hair behind her ear, "but very soon. I'm thinking before the summer starts. I've got a friend that's already over there making it huge, and she's been a big help with processing all of this and taking that first step."

"Yeah? Do I know her?"

She shakes her head. "No, she's from Mason Pointe."

"I meant do I know her music, Lainey."

A laugh escapes her and that finally gets the Pearson sisters' attention. "What are y'all talking about?" Katherine speaks up.

Lainey takes a deep breath before telling them about her plans to leave in a few months.

"I think that's amazing. Please take this in the best way," Izzy starts, "you are much bigger than this small town. You were *amazing* up there tonight and I hope more people are able to witness that."

Lainey blushes. "Thanks, that means a lot."

Katherine clears her throat and we all look at her. She makes eye contact with me for a split second and I wonder if Izzy or Lainey catch it. "Do it now, whether or not you're scared."

"I'm terrified," Lainey confesses.

"Then do it now while you have that fear," Katherine says confidently. "It'll drive you to shoot for things that you wouldn't think of aiming for. You've got us to fall back on to remind you just how great you are."

"You're going to make me cry," Lainey whispers. She reaches her hand over the table and Katherine grabs it. It feels like I'm interrupting a girls night for a moment but then Lainey grabs my hand with her free one. "You're all so good to me."

"We barely met," Katherine laughs.

Lainey sniffles for a moment. Oh, shit. I don't know how to deal with someone crying. I could barely handle my mom crying. But seeing someone else? It makes me feel uncomfortable and I don't know how to be there for them. Even with girlfriends I've had in the past, I wasn't the best of support. I want to be, though. I want to be that person that friends or a future partner can lean on in these kinds of situations.

I squeeze her hand for a moment and Lainey glances at me with surprise. "She's right," I say. I look at Katherine for a moment and smile at her. It's like it's just us for the next two seconds and I bask in it. I turn back to Lainey. "Do it scared. Do it afraid. But make sure that you just *do it*."

"Like Nike," Izzy chimes in. We all turn to her and laugh, not expecting that from her.

"Alright, I will. I'm *going* to. I can't wait." Lainey bites her lip for a moment before letting mine and Katherine's hands go. "Actually, do you mind if I go call my friend? She was hoping for me to reach out after my set to let her know how it went. I want to tell her that I'm ready for the next step. Nashville."

"Of course." Katherine speaks up for us all.

Lainey blows us all kisses before getting up and practically running to the back of the dive bar where employees are able to go.

"I think we just helped a super star in the making," Izzy says. "We better be in that documentary if she makes one of her life story."

"Izzy!" Katherine yells. I can't help but laugh. She turns to me and there are daggers in her eyes.

"What?" I smirk. Her eyes narrow and Izzy shakes her head.

"You know what I mean." Izzy waves her hand, dismissing her sister.

Katherine rolls her eyes. "I know, but it's the delivery of your message that I didn't like."

"Sorry, *mom*," Izzy teases.

Katherine pinches Izzy's cheeks.

"Ow!" she yelps.

"Mom is looking down at you right now," Katherine warns with a point of her finger. Izzy scoots her chair back.

"Jeez, don't say that. *That* is crossing a line."

"Sure," Katherine retorts.

"I'll get us a few more drinks," I finally say, breaking up the sister argument. I get up and they spew off their favorite dive bar drink orders. I take special note of Katherine's.

Honey cider with extra ice. Usually, they just hand you the can, so I make sure once I get to the bar to ask for that cup of ice. Once I'm back at the table, she perks up when I hand her the cold cider can and a cup of ice.

"Thanks, you didn't even try to pour it yourself." It's not a snarky remark. I can hint at the meaning of it. She didn't expect me to bring back the cup of ice separate from the drink. She probably assumed I'd pour it myself.

The last thing I'll ever do is pour a woman's drink without her seeing it.

"Nope," I say, popping the *p* with my lips. Izzy thanks me for her cranberry vodka and we settle back into the table.

The time passes quickly as we talk about nonsense. From memories of high school, to wondering if Camilla and Bennett will ever get married in the next two years, to trying to see how many shots the group of college kids across the bar will try to take. That last one was Izzy's bet.

So far, they're on the sixth shot, and I bet eight. Izzy lost at four and Katherine bet nine.

It's a fun night of feeling like I'm with genuine friends, relaxing and enjoying each other's company. My phone blows up a few times with clients wanting to know if I can work tomorrow despite it being Sunday and I try to get back to them as cohesively as I can. That's when I start to chug water versus ordering more beer.

By the time the clock nears 1 a.m., Izzy has already left. It wasn't planned and I could see the hurt in Katherine's face when it happened. But Izzy's girlfriend needed something urgently and came to pick her up.

I'm waiting near the door, watching for the Uber that's on its way. I offered to call Katherine one as well, but she declined. But now that my Uber is almost here, I wonder if she ever called herself one.

I feel someone behind me and turn to see Katherine there, nudging my back with her shoulder.

"You're a stiff cowboy."

"What?" I laugh, finally turning to look at her head on. She's a bit shorter than me, despite her five-eight frame. She cranes her head upward and I swallow hard. Her green eyes are captivating and there are some hints of amber that I don't think I've noticed before.

I've also never been this close to Katherine Pearson as I have this weekend. It's making my chest tighter at the realization that I'm *this* close to her. I can smell her sweet perfume and I close my eyes for a brief second, taking it all in.

God, I'm such a loser.

"You're stiff. Like all muscle-y." She giggles.

"I work a lot," I counter.

She shakes her head. "More like workout a lot."

"That's what I mean." I laugh. "Ranch work is hard work. Basically a workout in itself."

"Throwing bales of hay?"

"Not quite."

My phone pings and see that my driver is about to pull up. I walk backward toward the entrance and Katherine follows. Once we're near the front door, I completely forget about that stupid mistletoe.

"Oh, fuck," I say, uncalled for. Katherine looks up and eyes the mistletoe.

"Are you gonna do it? Are you gonna kiss me, Cowboy?"

The way the words flow out of her pretty mouth so smoothly gives me the confidence to grab her chin with one hand. My phone pings again, my driver is here.

I lean in and she gasps, eyes widening. I don't dare give her a chance to tease me again and ask if I'm going to kiss her.

I fucking do it.

SEVEN

KATHERINE

LANCE KING KISSED me like a fucking man.

The way he grabbed my chin, kissed me like it was the end of the world, and then left me breathless wasn't on my bingo card for tonight. Or in this lifetime.

I never thought that I'd feel so drawn to this man, despite the history I knew of him. Or the fact that we've been in the same town all our lives.

He finally leans back, but I get on my tiptoes to kiss him again and he does that fucking smirk that I'm starting to like a little too much.

I wasn't going to let the night end like this, me waving him off in his Uber while I sulked in my thoughts under the neon sign of the bar. If I was going to do something, it'd be tonight. Whether or not I let him take me to his bed, I didn't fucking care.

"My ride's here."

I look at him. Waiting. And I think he's waiting for my approval before he asks. *Here goes.*

"I'll go with you," I say confidently. His pupils enlarge for a second and my stomach does somersaults.

"Let's go then, Chestnut." The nickname is random, but I

don't think anything of it. I let him take my hand, pulling us out of *The Lost Cowboy*.

The Uber ride to his place is short, and I can't even remember the last time I've driven by his property. Or if I have ever driven by *at all*. His place is basically on the other side of town from where I live, so there hasn't really been any reason for me to drive out here.

Once the Uber stops us in front of his gate, he gets out to open it for the driver. He made it a point once we got in the Uber that he'd like for the driver to go past the gate to make sure I got out right near his porch steps.

Not sure why this had to be such a big deal to me, but it made me think *things*. Very dirty thoughts that made me want to pull him to my lips right there in the backseat.

"Have a nice night," the driver finally says once we're at Lance's. I'm about to reach for the door handle, but he makes a noise, like a grunt, which makes me stop.

Lance runs around the back of the car and opens my door. It's been a while since I've been treated this respectfully from a one night stand. Usually it's a quick process of getting us into their bed; no doors are opened for me or the whole nine yards. I thank him softly before he grabs my hand and we head up the porch steps. There's another house up further on the hill, it must be his mom's. I've heard about Lucy King many times and how she chose to stay in Alpine even after her husband passed.

It seems like I know more about the King family than Lance has ever told me. But that's also due to solely being with just one man for the majority of my life, Bennett. There was never really a time when Lance and I would be alone to even talk about the personal things. Why would I spend time trying to personally get to know another man in town when I had a husband?

It's all still new to me and it's been hard to transition from being newly divorced to navigating the dating scene. From hookup culture, to casually dating, to now wondering if I'm ready to seriously date someone again. I still don't know what category I'm in or if I'll just fall into the one night stand after tonight.

But something about Lance makes me think this won't be a one night stand situation.

"Need a glass of water? Anything?" Lance asks once we're finally inside the house. It's dark and I can finally hone into the sounds of the animals around us. Some crickets, and even a distant howling like someone's dog that's kept outside.

"I'm all good, but thank you," I tell him. I cross my arms over my chest, suddenly feeling awkward and unclear about what I should do with my hands or myself in general.

Get a grip, Katherine. Why are you so nervous?

I look down the hall where there are a few doors lined up and I wonder which one is his bedroom. He follows my gaze before turning back to me.

"Are you sure?" It's like he's reading my damn mind and I'm suddenly super grateful for it.

I simply nod and he gestures toward the hallway to let me lead the way. "It's the third one on the right."

I count the doors slowly in my head as I walk down the hall before we reach the third door. It's like I can't move my muscles and I swallow hard.

Fuck, I can't do this. The thought of having a one night stand with Lance isn't what I want. I want to stop that cycle. I want to—

"Everything okay? Do you need help opening the door?" There's a slight teasing tone in his words and it snaps me out of my thoughts.

"Y-yeah," I mumble. I grasp the door handle tightly, knuckles turning white. *God, he smells really good. Like amber and cedarwood with a hint of something else. What's his cologne?*

He's all I can smell and it oddly grounds me for a moment, so I breathe it all in.

I push the door open and it's like all my nerves have dissipated. There's a king size bed in the center of the room and some simple wooden nightstands. A corner of clothes piled up on a chair, which makes me smile because *same.*

A TV is on one side of the wall on top of a dresser. I don't know what I was expecting to see in his room, but it's a normal bedroom. And it calms me. No expectations.

I head to the bed and plop down on it, patting the space next to me. He shakes his head and stalks toward me. I crane my neck when he reaches me, pushing himself in between my legs. I make a sound as I lean back onto the palm of my hands.

"Katherine," he mumbles, so softly that I almost miss it.

"Lance," I say with a smile. My heart is pattering like a drum as he's leaning in closer, lowering onto his knees to be at eye level with me. I keep forgetting how fucking tall this man is as he runs his hand through his thick black hair. I reach out and run my fingers through it, pushing some strands behind his ear.

He looks up at me through his lashes and it's the prettiest sight. There's a wicked sense of...wanting to make him do whatever I ask. I've never done that before with a man. I've always been so submissive and letting them steer the conversations in sex.

But this time I want to speak up and I don't know why the hell this man in front of me is making me feel this way.

"Say what you're thinking, Darlin'," he says with a deeper voice that shakes through my core.

"I want you to..." I lift his chin with my finger, "pleasure me."

"In what way?" He breathes. He hooks a finger in the belt loop of my jeans. Just that motion alone makes my body jolt for him while his other hand rests gently on my thigh, his fingers slowly grasping with more force.

"Make me scream your name," I say.

"Already planning on it," he confirms.

"Eat me out until I'm begging you to just fuck me."

His eyes widen for a moment before he leans closer. His grip on my thigh tightens even further, and a gasp leaves my lips.

"You could've just started with that, sweetheart," he says simply.

As much as I was enjoying telling him what to do, the switch of him taking over doesn't bother me. Maybe if we continue this, I can practice being dominant more. He can ease me into it.

And that idea makes me wishful that this will be more than just a one night thing.

"Lean back," he says under his breath.

I follow his command and lean back. His hands are quick to unbutton my jeans and pull them halfway down my thighs. I help him get them off and he takes my shoes off just as quickly while simultaneously throwing both God knows where. His hands are back to my thighs and I suck in a breath. I'm ready to just get everything *off*. I wiggle to grab my shirt and yank it over my head.

"Eager," I hear him say as he grips the waistband of my panties. I say a silent thank you to past Katherine for putting on cute panties instead of something super embarrassing.

"Shut up and eat me out, Lance." I get the courage to bite back.

"You got it, Darlin'."

And without further ado, he pulls my panties down to my ankles and to the floor. I can feel his breath against me and my thoughts stall. Fuck, he's about to do this. *We're* about to do this.

I can't even express anything vocally because the next thing I know, his hands are gripping my hips and his tongue glides against my lips.

"Oh, God!" I scream, reaching down to grab a fistful of his hair. He moans in response and continues to work his magic with his tongue. Have I ever been eaten out this well? The fact that I can't even remember just shows how much I needed this from Lance.

"You're doing so well for me, Darlin'," he mumbles while we make eye contact for a second before he's going back down. There's a shift in his stance and that's when I feel a finger teasing my entrance.

"Lan—" I can't even finish my sentence before he slowly inserts his finger and his tongue glides against my clit. The feelings are overwhelming and I grip his hair, pulling him toward me. I don't fucking care if I rip his hair out and I don't think he minds either. I also don't care if his fingers leave bruises on my hip.

Before I know it, he's inserting another finger before fucking me so well that I don't even know if I could take more. If he's this good at just eating me out and fingering me, how is his—

A third finger inserts and I scream his name. He chuckles and the vibration of his voice shakes my body. I continue to grip his hair with one hand while the other grips the bedsheets, like an anchor. I'm drowning in him and he doesn't even know it.

"You almost there, Darlin'?"

"Y-yes," I croak out with a shaky breath.

"Good, 'cause you're going to come for me, and then again. And again. I want you to come so much that you can't think straight. That you can't even beg for more because you're so fucking satisfied."

His words echo in my head while he goes back to licking and sucking my clit while fingering me. It doesn't take long for the dam to break and I'm finishing on him. He lifts his head to catch me breathless before he dips his head again and continues.

I squeeze my thighs against his head, wanting him to stop but it feels too damn good. My head falls back in defeat and I look up at the ceiling and notice that there's some design on it. Wallpaper of some sort.

Another orgasm starts to surface and it breaks me from my thoughts before I'm screaming his name again. I lift my hips up, attempting to get away from him but he pins me down with his hand on my stomach.

He really is a man of his word.

I lift my head to look at him once more, wanting to curse him out for actually doing what he told me he'd do. But the way he looks at me, his lips shiny from my orgasms, shut me up.

"You ready for another one?"

I shake my head and he laughs. "No, Lance. You were right."

"Always am, Darlin'," he teases. "Come on, one more for me."

He's going to ruin me tonight, and I fully allow him to.

EIGHT

LANCE

A TEXT WAKES ME UP.

I furrow my brows. What the hell is she texting me about? Who the hell is Adeline?

It's been three days since seeing Katherine and it makes me wonder if she might know who Adeline is. It's also been a long three days of pining over a woman that I'm just starting to really get to know despite *knowing* her for all of my life.

And I can't even admit if it's really pining or just simple pheromones that are wanting me to fuck her. But I'm really enjoying the time of getting to know Katherine the way that I am. There is no room for assumptions, or 'he said, she said' to be in the way. She is telling me about herself on her own, and I am the same for her.

I quickly shoot back a response.

Before I know it, she's firing back a response before I can put my phone down.

LAINEY

1. I didn't say a specific horse. Just any. She's coming back for a little for Christmas and she mentioned riding and you're the only cowboy I know. I can introduce y'all.

2. She's the singer from Nashville. Addie Rose is her stage name.

Oh, shit. Addie Rose is a huge country star singer based in Nashville. I didn't think *she* was the one who Lainey was talking about. I was honestly assuming some small artist who was just singing at bars downtown or with a small record label, or honestly even independent. But Addie Rose has one of the best country labels backing her.

She went on an arena tour last year and sold out. She's supposed to be coming out with a new album very soon, so there's speculation that she'll have a stadium tour next. I'm surprised she's even coming back home for the holidays. I'm even more surprised that I know this much about her—what can I say? I love country music.

ME

I'm not really a cowboy. More of a rancher. But she can check out my horses and choose one she connects the most with.

LAINEY

Cowboy, rancher. Same thing.

I'll let her know. Thanks!

ME

I get up from bed and start my day. I have to check the horses before heading back to the Jensens, and oddly enough, it's a little past where Katherine lives. I wonder if she's home and if she'd mind if I dropped off coffee.

Stop, why are you going to bring her coffee? God, I have no idea what I'm doing. I scroll through my contacts until I find her number. I'm surprised I even have her contact in my phone as I create a new text thread.

ME

Are you home? It's Lance by the way.

KATHERINE MOORE

Yes... It's 5:30 am. Why are you up?

I widened my eyes for a moment as I read her name again. I knew something was off. I quickly go into her contact info and edit the last name back to her maiden.

ME

Just like everyone else in this town who has animals, I have to be up early to tend to them. Do you like hot or iced coffee?

KATHERINE PEARSON

Oh, right. Cowboy.

Iced. Two shots of espresso, please. And a bagel.

ME

Not a cowboy, but maybe I should start telling people I am. One coffee and bagel coming right up.

KATHERINE PEARSON

Is there a reason why you're getting me coffee?

I finish pulling a shirt over my head before I head to the bathroom to freshen up. By the time I'm done, I read her text again. As I make my way to the stables, I finally answer.

ME

Isn't that what friends do?

KATHERINE PEARSON

Friends don't make you come six times in one
night.

I almost trip going to the back where the feed mix and nutrients are. I start mixing them, trying to occupy my mind for the time being. How the hell do I answer that?

As I pass around the feed buckets to each horse, I respond.

ME

Fine. Isn't that what fuck buddies do? That
better?

I'm standing in front of Hershey's stall when I hear something. Not a neigh. A meow. I pull the stall doors open and Hershey isn't standing. He's lying down and there's a white kitten on top of his belly. They both stare at me like *I'm* the one out of place.

"What the hell?" I say loudly. I set the feed bucket down inside the stall. The white kitten meows loudly as if trying to claim its right to be in Hershey's stall. Hershey then huffs loudly as if backing up his new friend.

"Okay, you can stay. But I need to see if you're some little kid's Christmas present." They are silent as I walk up to them and kneel. Hershey is so fucking relaxed that it's making me confused and worried. Is he hurt? Or is he truly allowing a two-pound kitten to take over everything he does?

The kitten is a girl and she has no collar. I can bring her to the vet after getting coffee and see if she's chipped or not. But for now, I'll take care of her... But at this point, it seems like Hershey already is. I just don't want the kitten to get lost in this barn or the ranch property before any harsh winter weather hits.

"We're going to go on an adventure," I tell the kitty before holding her close to my chest. My phone buzzes, but my hands are full of this kitten as she nuzzles into my chest and continues to meow and even shake. She seems cold and it makes me sad to know that she might've gotten lost from her momma. I'll get some extra cat food and leave out a bowl tonight in case she comes looking for her baby.

I finish any more morning chores before bringing the kitten with me to the truck and heading into town. It's 6:15 a.m., and the vet opens at 7 a.m., so I quickly get coffee and bagels before heading to Katherine's. I forgot to text her back, so once I'm parked in front of her place, I check my phone.

KATHERINE PEARSON

We're not fuck buddies, Lance. That's so juvenile.

ME

I'm just the coffee delivery guy, huh? I'm here by the way.

Her response is rolling in, three dots appearing on my phone, but it never comes through. I instead see her porch light turn on and she's swinging the door open. She crosses her arms over her chest, and she's got a big smile on her face.

I hop out of the truck with the kitten in one hand and the bag of bagels and cup holder in the other.

"Hey," I call out before getting closer.

"Who's this?" she asks, eyeing the kitten. I hold the kitten a little higher on my chest.

"She was in the stall with one of my horses. She must've lost her mom last night and found refuge there."

Katherine's face softens for a moment as she takes in my words. She reaches for the kitten and I let her grab it. She cradles it against her chest and the kitten immediately moves upward and nuzzles her face into Katherine's neck.

"She's so small. Probably still needs to be bottle-fed for another week or two."

"I'm going to the vet once they open to see if she's anyone's."

"If not, make sure she gets any shots needed," Katherine states.

I nod. "Was already planning on that." Her eyes connect with mine and there's a pause, a comfortable silence.

She clears her throat before moving aside. "Come in, you can set the coffee down in the living room."

I head into her home and set the bag of bagels and coffee carrier on the table in the living room. Her home is warm and inviting, and the decor fits her personality perfectly. Some breathtaking landscape paintings fill the walls in this room while the beige furniture goes nicely against the white rug.

"Weird question to ask," Katherine says before setting the kitten down on a nearby chair before taking the bagel bag and rummaging through it for hers. They're already spread with cream cheese. One of the main reasons why I love Alpine Cafe, they make the best bagels and prepare them so it's ready to eat for those who are short on time.

"What's that?" I ask, grabbing the bag from her and pulling out my own. I bite into it and then take a sip of the caramel iced coffee I got. She takes a sip of her latte with two shots of espresso.

"Are you going to the vineyard this Saturday?"

I think for a moment and then remember what Ma said the other day. The Christmas party. At Stone Vineyard.

"I thought about it... Are you?" I ask her. She takes another sip of her coffee before biting into her own bagel.

"Morgan and Peyton will be there, so I will too."

"When are they coming to town?" Morgan is like a daughter to Katherine and Bennett, that I do remember.

"Tomorrow, actually. I'm planning to get lunch with them."

"That'll be nice," I genuinely tell her. She nods and takes a seat on the couch near the bay window overlooking her property.

"Bennett told me that he's building her a house, can you believe it? She's growing way too fast for my liking."

I heard some talks about Bennett building on the land that he and Camilla purchased, but it's all been through the grapevine. I didn't know the specifics, but Katherine is now filling in the blanks for me.

"I wouldn't know, but that must be hard," I offer. She gives me a warm smile. "She means a lot to you."

She nods. "Yeah, I've been there for her and Peyton through almost everything. I wish I could visit them more often instead of just waiting until they come back to Alpine."

"Why don't you visit?"

Katherine looks at the bagel for a moment before taking a bite and chewing on it slowly. Like she's processing her next few words. "I've never left Alpine. The idea kind of scares me."

This new information piques my interest. "Wait, you never left the town or just the state of Tennessee?"

She looks up and there's a shine to her eyes. Fuck, I hit a spot and I regret it. "I've obviously left the town and ventured off into Mason Pointe and whatnot, but I never really went further. It's like I'm rooted so deep into this area that I've never thought I have the option to go."

"Meanwhile, Bennett was deployed in so many countries," I say simply. I don't mean for it to have a bite to it and with the way she looks at me, I know she doesn't take it that way. Instead, she lightly laughs.

"Yeah, he got to see the world while I stayed willingly. God, this feels so silly even just admitting. Sorry."

I shake my head and walk closer to her. "That's not silly. Sometimes I regret not leaving like my brother did. He has a whole different life in Colorado and I wonder what would've happened if I did the same."

"Really?"

"Yeah." I nod. "I've got a bucket list I want to accomplish by the time I hit 40 or 50. Just a few places I want to travel to. I think I've been so stuck in this town too because of my mom. She needs me and I don't ever want her to feel alone. Even if I end up settling here, I want to take the chance to leave for a while and experience more."

Katherine's lip trembles for a moment and I place my coffee and bagel down on the table before grabbing hers and placing it down as well. I gently grab her hands and kneel to be face-level with her.

"What's wrong?"

"You should really work on that bucket list. Don't stay trapped here forever."

It's weird to say that this woman is thinking everything that I've been feeling the last few months—hell, the last few years.

"I was thinking of maybe crossing one of them off after Christmas," I say out loud. It was a thought this weekend that I want to come to fruition.

"Where to?"

I look up at the ceiling before landing on her gorgeous green eyes. "Smoky Mountains to start."

Her eyes bug. "You've never been? Okay, I have to admit that is *one* place I've been to! It's gorgeous during the fall time, and even better during Christmastime in the tiny town where they decorate to the nines!"

I smile, absorbing her enthusiasm. "That's what I plan to do. Go to the town, enjoy the Christmas lights, then maybe drive through the mountains and breathe in that fresh air."

"You're going to really enjoy it. What's next on your list?"

"Colorado," I say without missing a beat. "My brother invited me out there next Spring so I really want to take advantage of that invite. I see his family every other Christmas, but I've yet to visit them. My niece and nephews have practically been begging me over FaceTime for a visit."

Katherine's cheeks are red from how much she's smiling. "Looks like you're going to be tackling that list way faster than you anticipated."

"What about you?" I ask her.

"New York for Peyton and Morgan, but I don't know about anywhere else..." She nibbles on her lip for a moment, deep in thought.

I let go of her hands and place my palms on her knees. She draws in a deep breath. "You should make a list."

Her eyes narrow before she throws her head back laughing. "What? No! You have far more places you want to go to that deem having a list. I just have one place."

"*We* should make a list then. Add some of the places that are on mine to this list if you want to go there too." The words stumble out of my mouth quicker than I can stop them.

"What?" Her eyes widen.

I take full accountability of my words and nod. "Why not? Everyone else has been moving on with their lives and doing so much for themselves, it's time we do it too. We owe it to ourselves."

"Are you drunk? Or high? You sound insane." She laughs again.

"I'm sober as hell, Darlin'," I say confidently.

"Okay," she starts, "you're sounding a little too optimistic. What if a month from now we hate each other's guts? Or you no longer want to be friends with me?"

"I thought we established that we're not friends, nor fuck buddies."

"We're just..." she pauses for a moment, "*us.*"

"That's a good place to start, though. Right?"

I'm not sure why we're talking about this so soon. Call it chemistry, call it a fast burn, or whatever I've seen online about romance novels and why women love them so much.

It seems silly, but it also feels so comfortable talking about this with her. Like I've known her this way for years. I've known *about* her for almost all my life, but not this way. We're just two locals finally getting the time to get to know each other on a deeper, more personal level. An intimate one, too. I'm really starting to like the Katherine Pearson I'm getting to know lately.

"Yeah," she finally lets out, "*us.*"

NINE

KATHERINE

"WHAT'S WRONG, AUNT KAT?" Morgan asks while shoving a grilled cheese into her mouth. I grab a napkin quickly to brush off any crumbs from her lips, and Peyton laughs from the seat beside her.

We're at a new shop that just opened this fall called *Mint To Be Thyme;* it's a cute little sandwich-slash-soup type diner. She ordered a grilled cheese and tomato soup while I went with a turkey sandwich and yummy minestrone on the side. Peyton opted for a chicken and wild rice soup as big as Morgan's head.

"Nothing, baby," I say, focusing back on my food. Peyton clears her throat and I feel like a child under her watchful eye. She caught me.

"Really? You seemed so happy and chipper this morning, and now it feels like someone popped you like a balloon."

Damn, she got that right. "It's just—" I bite my lip. "I've been thinking a lot. Reflecting."

"On?"

"Yeah, on what, Aunt Kat?" Morgan chimes in. She looks so much like her dad and it breaks my heart at the same time as it mends it. He lives on through her every day and that's what all of us can ask for, really.

"On my life here. My purpose. What the hell I'm doing on this Earth."

Peyton's face turns serious. "Wait. Do we need to bring you to see someone? Like a professional? You should've called me earlier, I'm so sorry."

I wave my hand. "Oh, no! It's not like that, Pey! I'm serious, I'm fine. I'm just a little confused about how I've lived in this town for over thirty years and I've yet to explore the world."

She seems to relax a bit while Morgan isn't clued in on anything, happily munching on her grilled cheese. "Good, thank God. Just know I'll always be here for you if that ever becomes the case. Bennett, too, I'm sure."

"Yeah, I'm not so sure about that anymore. I don't think that's respectful to Camilla," I say as best as I can with a cheerful tone.

Peyton gives me a look. "Just because he's found someone else doesn't mean he doesn't care about you. We all care about you regardless of how things ended."

I shrug. "I'm not too caught up in that, Peyton. It's fine that he's moved on. I'm *happy* about it, Camilla is lovely. But I'll never have him cross boundaries just to make sure I'm okay. I'm not his priority anymore, she is."

"Wow," Peyton exclaims. She sits back on the chair and studies me. "That's very mature of you."

"Thanks," I mumble. Not really something I wanted to be congratulated on.

"I'm serious. You and Bennett dealt with a lot. More than any couple should. So seeing you say this is...genuinely admirable."

"Thanks," I repeat, but this time I mean it. "But, yeah, I want to get out there more. Meet more people, live my life. Sure, I can stay in Alpine and keep my house, but I don't want to be confined to this town forever. I want to visit people. Visit *you*."

"We'd love for you to visit. Right, Morgan?"

She nods with a mouthful of grilled cheese and soup. I lean over again and wipe the tomato soup off her cheek. This was something that Peyton always reprimanded me and Bennett for doing. We loved to clean up Morgan's messy eating habits. Peyton said it didn't help her learn and actually made it harder for her to understand that she's gotta do things on her own.

How can I stop though when she's like a daughter to me and I get that instinct to watch over her? I don't ever want children of my own, but Morgan is enough and gives me what I need when she's around.

That makes me quickly think back to Lance. It's such an odd thing, what's been happening to us the last week and a half. Do people really get this deep into things this early on? Clearly we're not really *dating*, but there's more to it.

Him confessing that he has a bucket list yesterday morning seemed deep and personal—like he never really told anyone about that before. It felt too soon, but I wanted to tell him that I'd love to go on adventures with him and help knock off a few places from the list.

Too soon. Most definitely.

"So, how are things? Studio going well?" Peyton pulls me out of my thoughts. I nod and cross my arms over the table.

"They're going really well, actually. My girls have a recital this Friday night and they're nervous, but so excited."

"That's amazing! I bet they're going to do so great. Do you want us to come watch?"

I shake my head. "No, you don't have to if you already have plans."

Peyton waves her hand. "Psh, we don't make plans when we visit. We go with the flow. Except for Saturday, that one is planned."

"Right, the party." I almost whisper it and Peyton eyes me.

"You're still going, right?"

"Please, come, Aunt Kat!" Morgan pleads with puppy eyes and tomato soup still on her lips and cheek. I laugh before leaning in to wipe again. She giggles and it makes me laugh too. Her happiness is so contagious.

"I'll go for a little bit," I finally say.

"Perfect, I heard it's going to be a big one. Birdy is catering and helping decorate."

"She's great at that," I remark. She really is—she's got a knack for decorating and event planning. I'm surprised she hasn't thought of doing it as a side hustle.

"She is," Peyton agrees. "Bennett has also been building this little one's home. Have you checked it out yet?"

"No, not yet," I sigh. "I've been meaning to reach out to him about that, but I didn't want to bother him with the party being so close. And Christmas in general. Busy times." I wave my hand in the air.

"I'm sure he'd like to hear from you and see what you think of the progress that he's made so far. We're going to check it out later today. Why don't you come?"

I would love to, but I don't want to impose. It would be their time with Bennett, and he deserves that.

As if by some miracle the Universe heard my pleas for a reason to say no, my phone pings. I pull it out of my sweater pocket and see *him*. My cheeks burn and I quickly glance at Peyton before opening the text.

LANCE

Busy tonight?

ME

For?

LANCE

Lainey wants to play us a new song. And have a bonfire.

ME

Depends.

LANCE

On?

ME

If there'll be s'mores, duh.

LANCE

Obviously.

I'm here at the store right now getting the
ingredients.

ME

Good job, Cowboy.

LANCE

I aim to please.

ME

Is that so?

LANCE

six time wonder, over here. I plan to beat that
record, btw.

I slam my phone down after reading his last message and I'm for sure blushing. I can feel the heat travel up my neck to my whole face. Peyton eyes me for a moment before she's helping Morgan clean up her plate.

"Who was that?"

"No one," I say a little too fast, "just a friend."

"Do I know them?"

I can't lie to Peyton, but maybe I can give her a white lie. "No, she's a singer though. Asked me to come over tonight to listen to a new song she wrote."

Peyton smiles. "That's nice, you should go. Morgan probably wants alone time with Uncle BenBen anyways."

I breathe a sigh of relief at her words. "Yeah, I don't want to impose on Morgan and BenBen time."

"Uncle BenBen better have my pink boots ready!" Morgan chimes in.

"He probably has a new color," I say, wiggling my brows up

and down. Morgan smiles the biggest smile ever and claps her hands with enthusiasm.

I glance back at my phone for a moment as Peyton gets up to put our used plates away.

ME

So we are fuck buddies. Good to know.

LANCE

Hey, I only said it once. You're prolonging this.

ME

I'm not prolonging anything. It's enjoyable watching you squirm under pressure.

LANCE

I don't squirm, Darlin'.

ME

Then what do you do?

His response bubble with three dots pops up, but then disappears for a few moments and I can't imagine what the hell he's trying to type. Or if he's rethinking what he truly wants to tell me.

My phone pings and the text finally appears.

LANCE

I'll show you tonight.

I close out the text thread as Peyton returns to the table. "Ready?" she asks, Morgan already jumping out of her seat. I nod and get up as well, grabbing Morgan's hand. Peyton grabs her other one and we walk outside.

The weather is warming up a bit with the sun, but there's a slight breeze that blows through my hair. We're heading toward the parking spots where our cars are when Peyton turns to me, Morgan swinging our hands as she's lost in her own little world already.

"Good luck with getting ready for the recital this week, it was so good seeing you. I'll see you Friday night," Peyton says, pulling me into a hug. I release Morgan's hand and hug my friend tightly. I miss her every day, but know that New York is the best place she can be right now. Maybe one day, when she's ready, she'll move back to Alpine with Morgan.

Bennett is definitely hoping for that too, hence why he's working fast to build her house.

"Love you," I whisper into her hair as I hug her tighter. "I'll see y'all Friday."

I lean down and grab Morgan, wrapping her in a bear hug. She squeals from the sudden motion but hugs me back. "Love you, Aunt Kat. I'll tell Uncle BenBen you said hi."

"You do that, sweet pea." I laugh, calling her the nickname that Bennett usually does, and kiss her cheek.

"Alright, honey," Peyton calls out, starting to head toward the car. "We gotta make it back to his place to clean up before we see the progress on the house."

Morgan gives me one last hug before running to her mom. I watch them go before I head to my own car.

There's a newfound feeling of jitters I can't explain just thinking about tonight with Lance. Even though I'll be seeing Lainey too, it's what he's wanting to do *after*. God, I feel like a teenager! Like I'm a clueless virgin, unsure how to go about anything.

I whip my phone out once I'm in my car and look up some cute lingerie shops. Alpine has none and I don't dare walk into Marla's boutique looking for something as risqué as what I want.

There's a shop thirty minutes away in Mason Pointe...perfect. I click the directions and start my car, pulling out of the parking spot and heading there.

TEN
LANCE

KATHERINE LOOKS ABSOLUTELY stunning tonight under the bonfire glow. Her red hair looks soft, I want to run my hands through it. Or wrap my fist around it and *pull*. Either will work.

Lainey has been playing a few covers for us as we drank some whiskey. It's been getting colder in Alpine by the minute and it feels like we *might* just get that Christmas miracle we've all been hoping for.

I glance again at Katherine and she locks eyes with mine. We're across the makeshift bonfire and her lips curve into the smallest smile before she focuses back on Lainey. Our texts have seemed to get a little bit raunchier and raunchier the later the day went on. My phone buzzes and I pull it out, wondering who the hell is texting me this late. It's almost 10 p.m.

KATHERINE PEARSON

Guess a color.

I look up through my lashes to see her looking at me for a second before bursting out into a fit of giggles. Lainey is still playing her guitar, oblivious to it all. I type out a quick response.

ME

If you're talking about a color of what you're wearing underneath…white.

KATHERINE PEARSON

That's too eager, we just met.

I almost spit out the whiskey I just pulled. Jesus.

ME

Scratch that, then. No eagerness here except to taste you. So I'm hoping it's red. Or green.

KATHERINE PEARSON

You feeling the holiday spirit?

ME

I could unwrap you like a present if you'd like.

KATHERINE PEARSON

Intriguing. Tempting.

ME

Anything you'd like, Darlin'.

KATHERINE PEARSON

The answer is red.

Lace.

My pants tighten after reading those words and I know that I'm done for. I glance up again and Katherine is talking to Lainey as if she didn't just taunt me like this over text.

"Lance, want to finally hear that new song?" Lainey asks, shifting her position to face me. I nod.

"You know I do." Another pull of the whiskey bottle. "What's this one about?"

She looks at me for a moment and blushes. But it doesn't seem like the kind where she's shy, more like embarrassed. I raise a brow.

"Actually, you inspired it."

Katherine gasps and looks at both me and Lainey. She narrows her eyes at me, and there's this sudden charge of electricity that I can feel emanating from her. Is she jealous? And why do I think that's the hottest thing?

"I inspired it? How so?" I ask, taking another pull. I need to stop if I want to enjoy the rest of the night. I don't need whiskey dick ruining anything I wanted to do with Katherine. And thoughts of my father keep creeping in my mind.

But I'm not him, and I'm not a drunk. I put the whiskey bottle down closer to the fire, away from my reach.

"By wanting me to go to Nashville. You push me to do better in my career and it made me think of all the people who don't have that kind of support in their corner, but still desire to be more. Whether or not they stay in their small town. I feel very lucky to know you, Lance, and to have you in my corner."

It's heartfelt and deep and it pulls at my heartstrings. I swallow a thick feeling in my throat, and my eyes get misty; I don't know if it's because of my emotions or because the damn bonfire smoke is creeping into my vision.

"That's what friends do," I tell her plainly. She shakes her head and Katherine watches intently, as if she's suddenly super interested in our conversation. She's quiet while she studies us.

"Exactly. We need more friends like you, Lance," Lainey agrees with a smile. She strums her guitar and starts picking out a tune. It's sweet and soft, like a lullaby. She starts to hum along before starting the first verse.

It's about growing up in a town where everyone stays, but the writer wants to leave so bad. She doesn't have the option to until a friend comes along to push her to want more. It's a cute melody that I'm starting to sway to, so is Katherine. Her eyes are closed as she listens to the lyrics.

Lainey dives into the chorus and I choke up. The words sting and it makes me have the urge to really get this bucket list going. I don't want to be confined to Alpine Ridge forever and I deserve to see what's out there for me. Even if I end up hating it and settle down in this town for the rest of my life, at least I can say I tried.

The second verse comes and I feel a tear fall down my cheek, but I'm quick to wipe it away so no one sees. I hang my head low and find myself staring at the whiskey bottle. The song starts to remind me more of my mom, too. She loved my dad until his dying days despite what he did to her and her sons. She continues to love him even after he passed. You can see it in her eyes, her words, and her actions.

I don't ever want to put anyone through what my dad put my mom through. And I won't. But I don't want to leave Alpine Ridge while she's still here. It sucks admitting it to myself, but it's true. That's why this bucket list will help me figure out if there's more out there for me. It'll allow me to still return to my mom and take care of her. I could tell her about all the places I visit, too. She'd love it.

Lainey finishes up the song and looks at me and Katherine for feedback. We start to clap and Katherine does a cute little howl. "You were amazing!" she yells.

"Thanks, guys. Lance, I hope you enjoyed it," Lainey states, turning her attention to me.

I nod. "That was great. I'll always be here to inspire you," I tell her with truth in my words. If I could inspire her in this way, I'd like to continue to be that. Everyone needs support and inspiration, and if just me talking to her about how she deserves to try for Nashville and knowing her worth and talent, then that's enough.

"Thanks, Lance," she states. She looks at Katherine for input. She's quiet and fussing with her hands on her lap before she smiles.

"I really liked it. Felt from the heart. Kind of reminds me of myself and being too scared to leave Alpine Ridge."

It's like she took the words right out of my mouth. I lean in to better listen to her. She glances at me for a moment before inhaling deeply. Lainey gives her the space to talk and I appreciate it a lot.

"I know we barely met, Lainey, but your words pull out the thoughts that I've been ruminating on for months, maybe even years. That's something special and not something every artist can do. But you do it so perfectly without even trying. It can help so many people figure out what they want in their life and I truly hope you're able to get that when you leave us."

Lainey has tears in her eyes and she puts her guitar down and gets up to hug Katherine quickly. Katherine holds onto Lainey tightly, and they hug for a few more seconds. It looks like Lainey is whispering something to Katherine and I let them have their moment. She sits back down and grabs her guitar again, wiping the tears from her cheeks.

"I'm not leaving y'all, by the way. If I could take you both, I would. Adeline loves Nashville, but she's not going to stay there long term. She said that you get tired of the famous part of things. The glamor gets to be too much."

"I thought that's what you wanted?" I ask, recalling what she told me at *The Lost Cowboy* last week.

She shrugs. "I talked to Adeline. A few times, actually. She really wants me to visit her and get my career going, but she doesn't want me to be sucked into the dangerous part of that industry. She just wants me to write my music and get it out there. I've never really had anyone be *that* protective of me in that sense. Sometimes I forget that my music is an extension of me and I need to ultimately protect it as best as I can."

"She's a smart woman," Katherine states.

Lainey nods. "Adeline is one of the smartest women I know and her heart is pure. I don't know if Lance mentioned it, but she's coming back to Mason Pointe for Christmas. She'll be here Saturday night and will stay a week before she gets a head start on the release of her new album. I'd love for you to meet her, too."

Katherine's mouth opens wide in shock and she tries to speak, but nothing comes out. That's when I butt in. "She'd love to meet your friend, Lainey. Thanks."

She's finally able to gain her voice back and nods, clearing her throat. "Yeah, what he said. God, I need to work on my reactions if I want to meet her. I can't be this starstruck when she's in front of me."

Lainey laughs. "No, you can't be. She hates being the center of attention, the complete opposite of me. She goes on tour because she needs to promote her work. She'd rather be holed up in a studio writing her heart away instead of being stuck on a tour bus."

"Complete opposite of you," I agree. Lainey wants it all, but now she knows she can't without a price. I just hope she's able to keep her head up while she goes through those motions. I have no doubt she will blow up the moment she sets foot in Nashville. Especially with Addie Rose by her side? She'd be unstoppable.

"It's getting late," Lainey finally says. "How about one more original Lainey Alpine?"

I pause for a moment. "Is that going to be your stage name? You never used that before, not even at *The Lost Cowboy*."

She nods, a smile stretching across her face. "Can't deny my roots. Alpine will always be in my blood, no matter where I go. *Y'all* will always be with me, wherever I go."

The moment is heartfelt, so I get up and sit closer to her, giving her a side hug. God, I'm going to cry again. Katherine decides to get up and sit on the other side of me, laying her head on my shoulder. Her hand goes to my thigh and I rest my palm on top of hers and our fingers interlock.

Lainey strums her guitar and we're all sitting on a small log, like critters trying to get warmth in the winter time.

The tune is delicate and very country. She whispers to us before she starts singing that this one came to her in a dream the other night and she couldn't stop writing it. It's called *My Roots Follow Me*.

A tear immediately falls again past my cheek and Katherine

squeezes my hand. We've all got our roots planted deep in Alpine Ridge—we can't change it, just something we have to live with.

Despite the obstacles, the challenges, and the highs and lows that I've encountered in the 37 years of my life here, I'm so fucking thankful that this has become where my life is. Because it brought me to this very moment with Lainey and...Katherine.

And I wouldn't change it for a damn thing.

ELEVEN

LANCE

KATHERINE OPENS her front door and we stumble inside. Just like that morning when I dropped off bagels and coffee. She's added some Christmas decorations here and there since then, but there's no tree. I almost ask, but that's not why we're here.

No small talk. No trying to get to know each other. The feeling of wanting to strip each other's clothes off was heavy tonight. After Lainey finished her songs, we ended the night with a few more covers and then she was ready to head inside. Katherine wouldn't loosen her grip on me though—the whole time.

It was such a strange circumstance, her not wanting to let go even after Lainey packed up her guitar. Her grip wasn't that strong, but I wasn't going to move if she didn't want to. We stayed on that log for a moment longer until Lainey made moves to head into her place. It would've been strange to hang around the back of her house without her present, so that's when we finally got up, hands still entwined.

I offered to drive Katherine home and she didn't hesitate to say yes. The drive to her place was comfortably quiet, just listening to some old country music and enjoying the backroads. She still didn't let my hand go, throughout the whole drive.

It wasn't until I parked the truck that I turned to look at her and her bright green eyes were on me, the moon above us casting the most beautiful glow on her fair skin. Before I could ask her if I could walk her to the door, she unbuckled her seatbelt and practically jumped to me.

I pulled her closer, hands in her hair, and her soft lips tasted like peppermint.

"Lance," she moaned, so softly I almost missed it.

"Inside?" I said with a shaky breath, and she nodded, letting me unbuckle my own seatbelt. We stumbled out of the car in a flash, and now she's taking my hand and leading me through the house like she's on a mission. To be fair, I am too.

I've never wanted anyone like this in so long. There's a fire in my body that is wanting to touch her all over. Hear her scream and moan and thrash underneath me.

She leads us inside the bedroom and wastes no time to plop onto the bed. I grab her waist, holding tightly as I lean over and kiss her forehead. It's delicate and intimate, not what we're going for tonight, but it's something I really wanted to do. When I pull away, her eyes are sparkling and she bites her lip.

"Lance," she says again, giving me damn tunnel vision. I can only focus on her. I could easily be in an alleyway right now or one of my barn stables by the way I'm so concentrated on just *her*.

"Katherine," I whisper back. The room is dark, except for the faint glow of the moon peeking through the curtains near the huge window across from the bed. Her property is on a huge plot of land, so even if we did have the lights on, no one would know what we'd be doing.

And I plan to do a lot of things to Katherine Pearson.

My hands glide down to her thighs before she grabs and brings them to the waistband of her jeans. She then wastes no time pulling her shirt over her head.

The ruby red lace makes me stuck like a deer in headlights.

Fuck, she's enchanting.

"Like what you see, Cowboy?"

"Very much so, Darlin'."

She giggles and it's like music to my ears. I want to drown in her, in every way. To play fair, I pull my own long sleeve off of my body and she revels in the sight. Her eyes trace lines over my body and I shiver, feeling goosebumps rise all over my chest. She's not even touching my skin and she's making me react this way.

"Can I?" she asks, sitting up taller and hovering her hands in the air. I nod and she touches my chest lightly. My skin jumps for a little before my nerves calm and she places her palms flat on my skin. She explores my chest with her hands. I see her swallow for a moment and I can't help but smirk.

"Like what you see, Darlin'?" I ask, repeating what she said to me. She nods and licks her lips.

"I like it a lot," she answers. Her palms continue to rub all over before I grab her wrists. She looks up at me quickly and I kneel down in between her legs. I'm quiet as I place her hands to her sides and start to unbutton her jeans. She inhales quickly, her body reacting so well to me. I toss the jeans on the floor before taking in the sight of the red lace panties she's wearing.

Like a fucking present just for me. Wrapped and ready to dive into. My fingers play with the lace waistband and she shivers.

"Fuck, Katherine. I have some very dirty fucking things to say, but also some that shouldn't be said."

"Shouldn't be said? Like what?"

I pause.

I don't know her dating history—I don't care for it. But all I know is her and Bennett, and the way things ended. I don't know the intricate details of it all, she can tell me when she's ready, if she even wants to.

I don't blame her if that's a chapter in her book she doesn't want to revisit. But my feelings aren't just all sexual right now and I want her to know that, so I take a deep breath.

"I can't believe a man let a woman like you go," I start. "I can't fucking comprehend it, I just can't."

Her legs close, tightening around me and I look up at her. She's smiling, but there's something else. Pain. Hurt. And comfort.

"I'm not *that* great, but this makes me feel better."

I shake my head. "You deserve a man that worships you. Crawls to you. Gets on his knees for you."

She looks at me for a moment before she half smiles. "Looks like you're one step ahead of the rest then."

I stay kneeled, not daring to move after she just said that. If she wants me to crawl to her later on, I will. If she commands me to do *anything*, I just might.

"What do you want me to do?" I ask, waiting.

Her eyes study me for a moment before she grabs the waistband of her panties and pulls them down until they're near her knees. I step back, thinking she'll finish taking them off.

"Take them off," she says. I listen immediately and pull them down her knees, off her feet, and toss them next to her jeans. "Now, do to me what you did last time, but better."

I raise a brow and grab her thighs, *hard*. "Better?"

She nods with a glint in her eyes. "Better," she repeats.

"Be careful what you wish for, Darlin'," I announce before moving my palm to her lower stomach and pushing, causing her to fall back on the bed with a huff from her lips. Her thighs shake a little, tense. "Good girl."

Her legs tighten around my torso as I trail my fingers *slowly* along her legs, her inner thighs, until I'm barely brushing the skin of her lower belly, right over her pussy. Fuck, my pants tighten and I need relief.

"Quit teasing and just do it," she moans from above. I slap her thigh, hard.

"Can't tell me to do one thing, then ask me to do another. I'm going to give it to you better. And then harder."

"Harder?" Her voice is faint, and her body stills as I trace random outlines on the lace.

"Mhm," I hum. "You know how."

"Fuck, Lance," she whispers. Before she can start commanding me to do more or even shit talk me even more, I'm burying my face in her pussy. I lick her clit, causing her whole body to jolt. My tongue knows exactly what to do to pleasure her, even though I've only explored her once. It feels like we've done this in every lifetime, but that thought alone calms me. I can have more nights to explore *every* inch of her body after tonight.

And I plan to.

"Lance!" She screams as I dive my tongue into her, gripping her thighs even harder. I can barely breathe, but I'll gladly pass out like this. Let the firemen find me unconscious and buried in her pussy, please.

"Scream my name again," I groan, pulling up for air. Fuck, it's like I'm purposely drowning myself and I couldn't care less.

She listens so well and screams my name as I dive back into her, licking and sucking every part of her pussy. She convulses and her thighs tighten around my neck, choking me, but I persist. Katherine is so close to her release and I can feel her, so I put more energy into getting her there. My cock is stiff, needing her lips or her pussy on it. I'll take either, to be honest.

"Lance, I'm going to—" She moans and I suck her clit before pushing my tongue into her once more and that's when the pressure builds and I feel her release. I *taste* her. Something I didn't know I could enjoy so fucking much until now. I don't stop tasting her, taking it all in, even when her legs are shaking and she's grasping at my hair tightly. If she continues, she'll for sure pull out some strands, but at this point, I don't care.

I move my hands to insert a few fingers into her wet entrance and she jumps, leaning up. I look up from underneath my lashes and see her mouth in an 'o', her fiery red hair a complete mess, and her hands gripping the sheets.

"No, please, I can't," she begs.

"You told me you needed better," I mumble before diving back in. She squeals and squirms beneath me and I twist my fingers inside her to hit the spongy spots that are her most sensitive.

"I-I know," she states breathlessly. "Just didn't t-think that it was going to be like this," she mumbles.

"You came more times the last time we found ourselves like this. You can do it," I praise her.

"This time," she breathes out, "is different. And you fucking know it."

"No," I respond before licking her clit once more and pulling up. "I don't."

She's quiet for a moment, despite her body doing all the talking. "You're lying."

I pause, chuckling. "Maybe. Maybe not."

"Oh, you little sh—" she starts but then screams my name once more when I flick my fingers up and continue to finger fuck her into silent rebellion.

Before long she's dripping all over my face—*again*—and her body is spent. But I'm not done with her yet and she knows it. She sits up, leaning on her elbows, and looks up at me once I'm standing. I unbuckle my belt and toss it to the floor. For a split second I think about tying her wrists up with it, but I want to take things slowly in *that* department.

I kick off my boots before going for my jeans. Her eyes watch my fingers unbutton them before they glide down my legs and I step out of them. She bites her lip and I raise a brow, waiting for her to tell me what to do next. I'm all hers for tonight—whatever she wants me to do, I'll gladly oblige.

"There's a condom in the bedside table," she finally states, motioning to the table to the right of me. I nod, heading over and pulling the drawer open. I notice there's not much content inside here except for some chapstick and a few condoms. Don't know why I thought she'd have a vibrator or something similar in there. Maybe it's in the one on the other side of the bed. I grab one before returning to her.

I pull down my boxers, my cock springing out, and her eyes

don't move from it. I begin to stroke it, making sure she's watching as I gather saliva in my mouth and then spit it out slowly onto my cock. She nibbles on her lip as I stroke my cock a few more times, hanging my head back and groaning.

"I want to taste you, please," she speaks up. I nod, and then get closer to her. Her lips perfectly align to the height of my cock and she doesn't even need to crane her neck. Perfect.

She licks her lips once more before leaning and taking my tip. I hiss from the contact and accidentally thrust into her mouth a little.

"Fuck, sorry," I mumble, attempting to back off, but she shakes her head and moans, grabbing my waist and pulling me into her further. Her mouth is doing wonders for my cock and I'm already close to coming—how embarrassing.

"Shit, I'm so close, Katherine. Your mouth feels incredible. Keep doing that with your tongue," I say to her, closing my eyes again and letting my hands grip her hair, pushing my cock further into her mouth and down her throat. She motions, as if she's adjusting with the length and trying to hold her breath. I let her move me how she wants, but I keep my grip on her hair.

After a few more seconds, I'm there and it feels so good. My cock pulses inside her mouth and I moan, letting it fill her mouth. I pull back a little so just my tip is in her mouth and she can breathe again.

"Take it all, Darlin'. Every. Last. Drop." My words are breathless and I groan again as she licks my tip before swallowing it all. My grip loosens on her hair and she sits back.

"Come on." She motions for me to come to her. She's wiping her mouth and I grab the condom that must've fallen and begin to unwrap it. My cock is still so fucking hard, so I hope it stays this way even after she drained me.

I'm quick to put the condom on and get on top of her. Her chest is glistening with sweat and I immediately take her lace covered breasts in my mouth, one at a time.

She moves a little underneath me and she's unclasping the bra before pulling it off and throwing it who knows where. I return my mouth to her breasts and suck on her nipples before she's begging for more.

I line my cock up with her entrance but she pauses for a moment and I look at her.

"I know we're using a condom and all but I just gotta tell you that I'm all clear. Just have to put it out there."

I nod. "Me too," I tell her. She smiles and wraps her legs around my waist to pull me closer to her. I can't stop myself and she can't either. My cock slides into her so easily and I hiss out loudly.

"Still so fucking wet for me, huh? You like my cock this much?"

"Yes, Lance. Fuck me. Make me come again. And again."

I wait no further to push my whole length into her and she winces before moaning loudly. Words of praise spill out of my mouth as I fuck her deeply. The world outside becomes quiet and I'm fully focused on this moment. Her green eyes are watching me, even when she's screaming and thrashing underneath me. She doesn't break eye contact, not even once.

This moment seems to be veering off into a more intimate moment, but I don't mind. It's what I prefer. Casual sex leaves out so much. Intimacy with just eye contact alone and being so focused on one another makes for the best orgasms, in my opinion.

"Fuck, Katherine." I groan when I feel an orgasm ready to take over.

"Come for me, Lance," she whispers as her pussy tightens around me and I can feel her close too.

I thrust faster into her and before I know it, we're both reaching our orgasms and our bodies shake as we come. I'm breathless, spent, and ready to sleep.

"That was—" Katherine groans when I drop on top of her, but making sure not to crush her. She continues to have her legs wrapped around me as she starts to run her fingers up and down my back.

"God, that feels so good," I moan. "Don't stop." I bury my face into her neck.

"Stay the night," she says softly. I lift my head to look at her for a moment and she's watching me for my response. She's scared that I'll say no, I can feel it. I can see it written all over her face.

I can't say no to her. I don't know why, but I can't.

"I'll stay."

TWELVE

KATHERINE

THE SOUND of Lance snoring next to me brings me peace for some odd fucking reason. Usually, I don't like men disturbing my peace—especially if they stay the night and snore. But his sounds are soft and not at all eardrum shattering.

It also feels *really* nice just having him in my bed. The warmth he provides during this colder week is like having my own personal heated blanket. We cuddled for a good while after we had sex and then we knocked out, our bodies spent.

I roll over and try to be as silent as I can possibly be while I get up and head to the bathroom. A hot shower to relax my muscles sounds really good right now. I look back for a moment, watching the rise and fall of his chest before I head into the bathroom and turn on the shower. The steam fills the room quickly and I take my time lathering soap all over. My legs are sore from all the tension and shaking last night. I'm going to have to take it slow today at work if I want to survive.

I've got a few classes this afternoon before we do a dance rehearsal to make sure everyone knows their place and routine before tomorrow night.

The nerves are already getting to me and I'm their *teacher*, so I can't imagine how all the girls are feeling. The hot water feels good against my head, as if it's washing away all of my anxieties and worries.

I'm quick to get ready in the bathroom before entering my room with the towel wrapped around me. Lance is sitting on the bed, putting on his shoes, when he looks up.

I head to my dresser to pull out some clothes. I don't feel uncomfortable with him sitting behind me, and especially after the things we did last night, I don't think I should be embarrassed to change in front of him.

As I pull on my clothes he's walking around, cleaning up the area. It's a nice gesture and I thank him softly.

"You want some coffee or anything?" I ask after a moment.

"I'm okay. Thanks, though," he finally responds from the door. I turn fully dressed and nod. His hair is unruly, but he still looks just as attractive as ever. His phone pings and he pulls it out, taking a look at it. His brows scrunch.

"Everything okay?" I ask, stepping closer. He nods before tapping a response and looking up.

"Ma wants me to help her put up some more decorations outside her house. I completely forgot to decorate my own place, so she just reminded me."

I laugh. "I mean, have you seen my place? The weather is starting to get cold, but it's not really giving us those Christmas vibes to want to decorate fully."

"You still need a tree," he agrees. I smile.

"I do, but I want a real one. Haven't had time to get one, unfortunately. I've always had a fake tree, but last year I was wearing the slipperiest socks in the world, tripped, and fell right on it, bringing the whole damn thing down with me." He laughs before I continue. "Since I don't have a tree anymore, I promised myself this would be the year I get a real one. But, I have a day full of classes and then the dance rehearsal."

"Busy day," he states.

A thought comes to me. "You can come tomorrow, if you'd like."

"To the dance recital?"

I nod.

He shifts his stance before leaning against the doorway, crossing his arms over his chest. "I don't want to intrude. It's your job and your space."

"I'm inviting you, Lance," I argue. "Plus, I'd like you there. As much as I appreciate Morgan and Peyton being there, I don't know if their presence will calm me."

"And mine will?" His voice goes soft.

I step again to close the distance. I crane my neck to look at him and he swallows. His eyes are so pretty, I could get lost in them.

I've lost myself in blue eyes for over half my life, but *these* blue eyes are something special.

Something new and exciting. Warm and comforting.

"Yes, it will," I plainly state.

He takes a deep breath and nods. "Okay, I'll be there."

I smile before he steps back and we both walk to the front of my house. I give him a kiss on the cheek and his face reddens for a moment before he's out the door and into his truck. My eyes never leave it as he backs out of the property. It's not until a rooster screaming in the distance breaks me out of this trance.

"Fuck," I shout before slamming the door and getting ready for my busy day.

THE GIRLS DID SO good tonight during the rehearsal and it eased my mind a ton. They perfected the moves, the music didn't stall, and my heart rate didn't cause me to go into cardiac arrest.

It went *too* well, which kind of scares me. If today went this well, does that mean tomorrow will be a shit show?

That's the main concern I have while driving home until my

phone pings and it's my sister texting me. I'm thankful for the distraction as it pulls me away from my current worries.

IZZY

I can't make it tomorrow. I'm so sorry.

There we go. The second shoe dropping. My heart stops for a split second and I fear this might be my last day on Earth if something else happens. I try to maintain composure while driving, I only have a mile left until I'm home. I'm absolutely against texting and driving, but my nerves won't let me put the damn phone down. I type out a quick response, I'll use the voice-activated assistant with my next text.

ME

What happened? Are you okay?

The voice automated assistant reads off her text as I take a turn.

IZZY

Twisted my ankle going UP the damn stairs.
Haley has been icing it, but it hurts to walk.
She's scared it's something more serious and
wants to take me to urgent care tomorrow.

Fuck. That's serious and not her fault at all if she has to miss the dance recital. I recite out a response for the assistant to send back to my sister.

ME

It's okay. Ice up and rest, please. I'll see you
Saturday, hopefully.

Izzy doesn't respond by the time I pull into my property. There aren't any decorations outside yet, I haven't had time, so it's basically pitch black as I hop out of my car. Sometimes I wish I had a dog or a cat—it gets lonely coming home, especially at this time. No one to greet me once I come inside.

The house is quiet and memories of this morning come to the forefront of my mind.

Lance.

I haven't heard from him all day and even though we aren't really on a daily texting basis, it's odd to not at least to get *some* kind of notification from him. As I get ready for bed, filling and turning on the tea kettle, I pull out my phone.

Our last text thread was from the bonfire. I didn't even ask him what his plans were for today. I was so involved in my own stressors with the dance recital that it didn't even cross my mind. All that he told me was that his mom needed help decorating, but I can't just show up unannounced, banging on the door of his mother's house. *That* would be weird.

I settle for a text instead. The tea kettle clicks off and I pour the boiling water into a green tea mug that has cute little red bows all over it. I got it for a buck at one of the nearby garage sales. I love bargain hunting when I have the time to do it.

ME

How did the Christmas decorating go?

It's almost eleven, so I don't expect him to answer me. I send my sister one last text to ask her to keep me updated on her ankle before heading to the bedroom and hopping into my comfy bed.

I glance one more time at my texts, deflated that the one person I really want to talk to isn't answering me. I could call him, but are we on those terms? God, it's been so long since I've dated.

We're not dating, but this is the closest I've gotten to it in a long time. We're not hooking up, that's for sure. It seems more emotional and intimate than that.

I opt for a book to fill my time as I wait up just in case he texts back, if he ever does at all.

THIRTEEN
LANCE

EVERYTHING THAT COULD GO WRONG, is going wrong, and it's really fucking up my day.

Hershey wasn't looking too good this morning and that brought on a fuck ton of stress and trying to feed him a little more medicine than usual.

He's nearing the age of *you know*, but I don't know if I'll be ready for that. I made sure to give him all the hay and kisses before I left for work. That's when even more shit hit the fan.

The Jensens were out of town yesterday, the one day I of course wasn't over there, and there was a freak accident that happened. All their animals were safe, except for one chicken. A coyote found its way onto their property and had the guts to go into the horse stables, spooking all of them pretty good before it moved on to the other areas of their ranch. They have watch dogs and all, but I guess they just didn't account for that one chicken that was out of the coop.

So, I had to calm down the horses and make sure they were okay enough to leave their stables for some rides later that day. The Jensens primarily use their horses for trail rides and riding lessons. It's a little different from the other ranchers that primarily board horses for rich families around the state.

It was already nearing 4 p.m. when I left their property and had a to-do list a mile long that I still had to conquer. The dance recital is at six-thirty and I am determined to make it.

Oh, yeah, that reminds me that I have to fix my phone. While checking on Hershey this morning, I didn't even have time to check my notifications before he got spooked from a plastic bag that somehow got into his stall and pushed me with his hind leg. Because of that, my phone went straight into the water bucket. Turns out it was Snowflake, the barn kitten that I decided to keep for the time being and obviously name. I don't know how she got a plastic bag, but it did some damage to my day.

Just. My. Luck.

With the Jensens being my only work for today, it was easy to get by without a phone, but now I don't even know if I'll have time to get it fixed before the recital. Hopefully by the time I make it, she'll see me in the audience and know that I'm there.

After a short drive, I'm parking in the lot for the Christmas tree farm that's set up in the middle of town. I scope out some of the trees quickly to see which one she'd like the best. It's really busy today for some reason and it's making my anxiety heighten as I check my watch and see that it's already nearing 5 p.m. I still have to get her damn flowers from Rose's shop.

After she told me the story about wanting a real tree this year, I made it my mission to get one for her. I can keep it in my truck while I'm at the recital and then help her set it up after.

If I can make it on time.

My heart is racing and my palms are starting to sweat as the time ticks away. I go and find the owner of the Christmas tree farm to tell him which one I want.

Once I get the tree tagged, he veers me into a line that's basically a mile long so that I can pay. Where the hell did all these people come from? Shouldn't half of them be at the recital? I get that Alpine is becoming a more well known town, but I need to pay for my damn tree, *now*.

I'm tapping my toes frantically as I wait in line and see from my peripheral the owner getting my tree ready for transport. At least he's doing his best to be as efficient as possible with the trees.

As I near the register, I over hear the cashier talk about technical difficulties and having to write down credit card numbers on a notepad to manually charge people if they didn't have cash.

Fuck, I don't have cash. And that's why it's taking forever. I glance at my watch once more and my eyes widen. Shit, shit, shit. It's 6:15p.m.

I don't know how long dance recitals go, but I don't think they're three or four hours long, which I really need.

I'm late, I don't take pride in being late.

The line finally dissipates and I get to the older woman manning the register. I whip out my card and hand it to her. That's when I realize that she's taking longer because she must have some joint issues. Her hands are slow to grab the pen and write down the numbers.

"I can do it," I offer, leaning closer. She looks up and smiles, shaking her head.

"Oh, no, sweet boy. I can do it. Thank you though." She returns to slowly writing down my numbers. She then flips the card over, her hands shaking and it drops to the floor.

Oh, God. As much as I feel for her and her joint problems, I have a recital to get to. I almost round the little table she's stationed at to grab the card but she's already turning and leaning down to get it.

"Clumsy old me," she jokes before she grabs the other numbers needed and then hands me the card again. "Thank you for shopping with us. Expect the charge tomorrow morning!"

I thank her before hightailing it back to the owner where he's ready to load my truck with the tree. We do it quickly and I've got spare ratchets to secure it to the truck. I thank him before I get in, ready to speed my way out of here, tree in tow, to the small theater Katherine rented out for the recital.

But when I turn the key, the engine stalls, and my eyes widen.

"No, no, no." I turn the key again and it stalls again. I pull the key out, not wanting to damage the engine even further, and get out of the truck. My eyes scan the lot and I see a few other guys walking about with their partners or families.

One of them should have jumper cables.

I call out to one of them and thankfully, they do have a set. It takes about fifteen minutes to get my truck going and I thank him a million times. I would've offered a damn horse with how much I needed it.

The cabin lights flicker and I groan, not wanting to deal with *one* more fucking thing. That's when I see the clock. Seven-fifteen.

I lean back and my head slightly slams into the headrest. Fuck. I feel defeated and my whole body deflates from the shit show that happened today. That's *still* happening.

All I know is that I promised Katherine that I'd be there, and I'm not. Not by choice, and she doesn't even know. She probably thinks that I purposely flaked and I fucking hate it.

I can't even call my mom to rant about this. Or my brother.

"Fuck!" I slam my fists against the steering wheel and try to not lose my cool. And by cool, I mean crying. Because I'm not my father, an angry man. I know how to control my temper. But there are days where I can't control my sadness and things get so hard that instead of anger, I get frustrated and I start to tear up.

Call it weak, but I'd like to think real men know when they need to cry and aren't afraid to own it.

I take a few deep breaths and start to make a list in my head of what's going *right*. So far, I've got a short list: the truck is working fine again, I've got a tree, and I was able to decorate my mom's place a little yesterday. So for today, I only truly have two things going for me.

Okay, what can I do right now to make it up to her? I can't just go and barge in midway into the recital. That would be real fucking rude. And what if it's just an hour thing? That means it's probably over and she's seeing who showed up. Fuck, fuck, fuck.

I hate disappointing people I care about. And I care a lot

about Katherine Pearson. I gave her my word and didn't show. Can't even text her an apology, how pathetic.

A thought occurs to me just then. I have her tree. *I have her tree.*

I put my truck in drive and head out of the lot and toward my place to pick up a few things before I head to hers. If she's there, then God, I deserve everything that's coming to me. But if she's not, I have some time to prep what I have planned.

I hope it's enough, because she deserves more.

FOURTEEN

KATHERINE

HE DIDN'T SHOW. I don't think it was the fact that he didn't show that pissed me off the most—it's the fact that he gave me his word.

I take people's word for what they are; it shows me who they truly are. After years of not being honest with Bennett and finally speaking my mind, I vowed to myself to always be honest and say what I mean—show up for people who I give my word to.

We weren't perfect, by any means, but there were some faults too with Bennett and him not giving me his word. I don't really stay stuck in the past, but Lance's actions tonight opened old wounds that were already stitched back, healed, and a faint scar.

No text. No call. Nothing.

Even though Morgan and Peyton showed, it didn't feel the same. There were some pre-show jitters that I thought could easily dissipate with him if he arrived early enough, so that alone made me feel even more nervous. It made me even more worried about him and it lasted throughout the whole damn show. I kept glancing out to the audience from behind the curtain anytime I could to see if maybe he slipped into the audience, but no, his seat stayed vacant.

Peyton tried to console me after the show with a huge

bouquet of flowers. I gave her a hug and smile, and then did the same with Morgan, before I told them that I just wanted to have the rest of the evening with myself. She offered to take me to dinner, but I kindly declined.

Driving home, I was still worried as hell alongside the anger that kept bubbling inside. Was he okay? I haven't heard from him since *yesterday* and that wasn't normal. I knew I should've listened to my gut and stopped by earlier today to see if his truck was on his property or something. *Anything.*

I briefly have the thought of trying to call him again, for the sixth time tonight, but I forgo it and head onto the driveway up to my place. That's when I see it.

Christmas lights decking not only the trees around the property, but wrapped around the porch railing and the shrubs on the flowerbeds out front. This wasn't my doing. I could only think of one person and he's standing on the porch steps with a little white thing in his hands. I try to squint to see what he's holding, but my headlights are too bright against the stark night and he's still too far to make out. I kill the engine and hop out, finally taking in his truck on the side of my house.

"Hey," he calls out. I walk to him and hike my bag up on my shoulder. My body is exhausted, as if it's finally releasing all the work I did the last few weeks and stress from today.

I don't answer him. How could I? I keep my head held high as I finally close the distance. That's when I see the cutest little kitten in his hands, it's the same one from a few days ago. I don't know why I thought it could've been a puppy, or like, an opossum. God, I'm blind.

I finally speak up, but not to him. "You're back already?"

He steps closer and holds the kitten out toward me. I grab it softly, its meows filling the silence around us. It's quick to want to be held even closer, so I oblige allowing it to crawl up on my chest and burrow its face into the crevice of my neck.

"Did you have time to bring her to the vet?" I finally ask, giving Lance a look. His face is full of concern and regret.

Good, he should feel bad.

"Yeah, she didn't like it one bit." He exhales a defeated breath, watching me for a reaction. We're having a normal conversation about a kitty, yet there are so many undertones waiting to erupt.

I raise a brow. "Still no mama cat around?"

He shakes his head.

"I put out some food that night to see if she'd come around, but nothing."

"Does she have a name?" The kitten meows and I caress her small body. She's practically the size of my palm, has to be at least five weeks old.

Lance looks at me for a moment before smiling, digging his hands into the front pocket of his jeans. "Snowflake."

My heart melts at the name and I coo at Snowflake like she's my baby. I even do the damn motion of bouncing up and down to calm her and her meows start to die down.

"She's perfect. White as snow, I'm glad you found her now before she got lost in the winter weather we're sure to have."

Lance doesn't reply, he just looks at me and then his face goes back to that sulking expression. I sigh. Time to get this over with. He'll probably yell a few things, I'll argue back, and then we'll either make up or hate each other for the rest of our days.

That's what I'm so used to, it's like second nature at this point. That's all I know.

"I wanted to apologize," he starts, and that surprises me, so I give him my full attention, despite my hands all over Snowflake. "It was a shit show today, I did my best to be there on time. Everything that could go wrong, did. I feel horrible and hope you know that I am a man of my word and it was like some damn force trying to disprove that."

I shift my balance from one foot to another. "I looked for you. The whole night."

He takes a step forward and I let him. I don't back away. "My phone dropped in one of the horse's water buckets this morning before I could even check any texts. Work was even busier than I anticipated, so I had no time to stop by here or even get a new phone."

"So why didn't you show up to the recital? I thought you didn't work that late," I point out. To make myself feel better, I threw a dig at him. "Thought you might've passed out at *The Lost Cowboy* or something and forgot about me."

The way he looks at me after is like I've stabbed him in the heart, twisting it to make it hurt. His brows scrunch and his pained expression makes me regret saying that.

"I'm not my father, Katherine."

Fuck, I messed up. I went too far. I knew he wasn't like his father, I just wanted him to feel the hurt I was in. But he wasn't Bennett and I have to keep reminding myself that. It was so easy to fall into an argument with Bennett, throw a few insults at each other where it really hurt, then walk off with a pissed off temper and even more broken heart and marriage. Every dig we threw at each other chipped more and more into our relationship until there was nothing left to chip at.

He sighs and looks up at the dark sky, the stars and moon illuminating my property perfectly. The Christmas lights he put up help too, I guess. It's like he's attempting to find the right words to say. I half expect him to start spewing off insults and walking to his truck.

"I didn't work late, Katherine. I had a few things I wanted to get before meeting you."

"What was more important than your damn presence?" My words come out with a bite and I don't really mean it, but the annoyance is starting to creep in again. Snowflake meows and I bet she can feel my increasing heart rate. I coo again and pet her bottom like a baby and she settles down again.

"This." He motions to the lights around my house. "I was going to pick up all of these lights, a tree, and then some flowers if I had extra time. They were so busy though and took all that time. I should've left, but I promised myself that I'd get those things before your recital."

"You didn't have to," I state plainly.

"You wanted a real tree," he counters.

My eyes narrow and I look around my front yard for this 'tree'. "Don't see one, so I guess you're not really a man of your word."

That's when he *laughs*. I stare at him incredulously. Is he really laughing right now? Guess I really did go too far and poked the bear a little too hard. And right now, I'm feeling more hurt *for* him. I shouldn't have brought up his father. It's a sore subject and I knew it enough to not say it. I was being petty, immature, and he didn't deserve that.

He nods toward his truck and I turn around. "It's in the bed. Didn't want to break in to put it up, although I did consider that idea. Wanted to set it up for you and everything. Got some decorations so you could enjoy that part, though."

"Shit," I whisper. I turn to look back at him and all he's giving me are *calm* and *forgiving* eyes. Not angry blue ones that I was so used to looking into.

God, I need to go back to therapy if I keep having these comparisons to my ex-husband. I've just never known anything else.

"I'm sorry," I blurt out. I take a step closer to Lance and we're cowboy boots to Uggs. I crane my neck to look into his beautiful eyes. "I'm so sorry I said that. I'm stressed and tonight didn't go as planned. Not just because you didn't show, but things didn't work like they were supposed to and it felt like the rehearsal last night was useless."

He doesn't hesitate to lift a hand and gently hold my jaw, caressing my cheek with his thumb. The motion is so soft and delicate that it's like a feather touch.

"It's okay, Chestnut. We both had horrible days and it just wasn't fair how the Universe wanted to torture us like this."

I smile and he does too. "What's with the nickname?" I finally ask. It's been bothering me since the first time he called me that.

He stills, then smiles before shrugging. "Chestnut horses have rich red coats. Your hair reminds me of them."

"A cowboy nicknaming me based on a horse's coat color? That's a new level achieved."

"Not a cowboy." He laughs.

I hold Snowflake closer to my chest and he glances down at her, dropping his hand from my face to scratch her behind her ears. She lets out the softest noise while purring like an engine in my hands. "She's probably the best Christmas present I could get," I admit.

"I'm glad you like her, but the tree was the present." He laughs.

Oh.

A laugh escapes my lips. "Oops, I swear I'm happy about the tree too. I always wanted a real tree."

"I know, I listen."

He does, and I think I can get used to it.

"You're not him, by the way," I announce. "I'm sorry I said that. I get so caught up in my head that insults seem to be my immediate defense. You didn't deserve that."

"It's okay," he says softly.

"No, it's not, Lance," I say with a shake of my head. "You're not him. You're not his mistakes. And you shouldn't be defined by his past, or *your* past, for that matter."

His eyes soften and his chest heaves in a big motion and he looks up at the sky again and exhales. The colder air causes his breath to fog.

To push my apology even more, I tell him in one slow breath, "The past is not a definition of your now, never was."

"How did I get so lucky?" he asks the sky. He then looks down and grabs my waist.

"I'm nowhere near a good luck charm, you might want to look elsewhere," I joke, rolling my eyes.

He pulls me closer and my core hits his. Butterflies immediately flood my stomach. Not only have we apologized like mature adults, we're willing to still be a support for each other. It's new territory that I'm growing fond of. I really like it.

He leans in to kiss my nose and then leans back before he kisses my lips. My eyes are shut, soaking in the moment. When he finally pulls away, his blue eyes are sparkling and my heart skips a beat.

"Don't need a good luck charm when we've got a mistletoe."

FIFTEEN
LANCE

I'LL HAVE to text Lainey and thank her for putting up that damn mistletoe at *The Lost Cowboy* tomorrow morning. Tonight, I'm going to make Katherine Pearson forget about her stressful day.

Hell, I'm going to make her forget her own damn name.

She tosses her bag to the ground while cradling the kitten before walking to the living room and sitting her down in a chaise near the window. I toss a set of Christmas lights I left on the porch, hoping we can bring the tree inside later tonight or in the early morning to start decorating.

But her green eyes are asking for something else. They're asking for *me*, and if I didn't give her what she wanted, then I'm useless.

"Come here," I say swiftly and she does so well in listening that she walks toward me. She wraps her arms around my neck and I pull her in by the waist, breathing her in.

Fuck, I hope she knows how much I need this. Need her.

"You didn't have to decorate my porch," she whispers.

My hands squeeze her waist and she wiggles underneath me, a smile breaking out. "That was nothing."

Her brow raises. "I wonder what *something* looks like then."

Without saying a thing, I lean in and kiss her. It's passionate, and warms the soul—an oddity for me.

"Lance," she moans in between kisses and I drag my hands down her sides until I'm leaning down to hoist her up from under her thighs. She squeals as she wraps her legs around my waist. I turn us around and head for the big white couch. The kitten is nowhere to be seen, which I appreciate. I don't need her seeing all the filthy things I'm about to do to her new mom.

"Say my name again, just like that," I ask nicely, dropping her on the couch and climbing on top of her, in between her thighs. She squeezes them around me and bites her lip, staring at me with those doe eyes that could ask for anything and I'd do it.

Need me to steal Santa's sleigh? I'm on it.

Her hands go to the hem of her shirt and before I know it, she's pulling it off. The sports bra underneath is black with white designs. Almost by instinct, I palm each of her breasts and take my time rubbing them until I feel just how achingly hard her nipples are.

She moans my name again and I black out. Well, not really. But that's the effect she has on me. My hands are quick to grab the bottom of the sports bra and pull it over her head. I place my mouth on her right breast, sucking and swirling my tongue over her nipple. Her moans vibrate against me and I grunt back, my free hand going back to her other breast and squeezing it.

I'm almost too enchanted in this moment and have to drag myself out of this fantasy when her legs tighten around me again. I lean up, a string of saliva leaving my mouth, connecting to her nipple. She grabs my face, making me look at her.

"I need you *inside* me, right now. No time for foreplay, I'm sorry." Her eyes are watching me, waiting for me to say...no? Is she fucking serious?

"I thought you'd never ask." I laugh, sitting up and getting off the couch to take off my own clothes. While I'm doing that, she is pushing off her leggings and panties. I grab the condom from my wallet and rip it open, rolling it onto my cock.

"Fuck, I don't know if I'll last long to be honest," I say, my body suddenly ready the moment that I look at her naked form. She's waiting so patiently on the couch and I take my time painting her in my mind. "You're so ethereal," I blurt.

Her cheeks turn red and she curls her fingers at me to come back to her.

Yes, fucking ma'am.

I hop back onto the couch and line myself with her entrance, grabbing one thigh to spread her even wider for me. She's intently watching the scene unfold as I push my tip and then my length into her. She hisses before I start to massage her inner thighs and then lean down to spit on her clit. Her body shudders.

"Fuck, Lance, you're so big." She moans. That does me in, causing me to push to the hilt, stuffing her. Like a damn Christmas stocking.

Just that thought alone gives me an idea. I look back on the other cushion right behind me and there the Christmas lights lay. *Hmm.*

"Katherine." I grunt, thrusting harder into her. She's moaning loud and has her eyes shut tightly as she concentrates on not letting go so soon. "Katherine, look at me," I say sternly, and she whips her eyes open. Goosebumps line her body and that boosts my ego. She loves it when I order her around. She might love to try to be in charge, but she seems to enjoy *me* telling her what to do much better.

"Yes, Cowboy?"

Fuuuuck, if I wasn't already so close, this would put me closer. *Much closer.*

"Give me your wrists," I tell her while reaching behind me for the lights. She throws me a quizzical look, but doesn't ask any questions before she's reaching her hands toward me. "Good girl," I say.

"Oh, fuck, don't say that." She laughs.

"Why not? I call it like I see it."

She smirks. "You're something else, Cowboy."

I wink at her before pulling the Christmas lights right in front of her to see. Her eyes widen.

"What do you plan to do with that?"

I don't respond, but instead, I show her. I pull her wrists closer to me and start wrapping her wrists with the Christmas lights. If an outlet was closer to the couch I'd plug these lights in and have her lit up like a Christmas tree.

"Bondage, wow, never done this before." She blushes.

I begin to pull the lights up and above her, bringing her wrists over her head. She twists a little, getting more comfortable, and I begin to wrap the rest of the length of the lights around her arms before setting the remainder off to the side of the couch.

"Keep them there," I order her and she nods. This makes my cock twitch and I'm ready to slam into her again. I line my tip up with her entrance once more and she takes a deep breath, eying me before I push inside her.

We waste no time getting into a rhythm again, her hips moving in unison with the way that I'm thrusting into her. She's tightening around me and I can feel her getting closer and closer. My thumb attaches to her clit and I rub it in smooth, small circles. Her hips rise with her arousal and I know she's going to come soon.

"Come for me baby, you can do it." I grunt while thrusting faster into her. She screams my name again and again and I swear that I've died and went to heaven with the way she says it. The way my name leaves her lips, it's pure ecstasy.

"Shit, so close—" I moan before she screams as well.

"Oh, God!" Her body lifts and I slam into her once more before she's coming and I follow right after. Our bodies are sweaty, her hair a mess. But she looks like a goddess, she always does.

I have just enough strength to pull out, tie the condom and toss it to the ground, and then untangle her from the lights. She's waiting patiently like a good girl and then once the lights are off, she's pulling me down on her. We're breathing heavy and her nails immediately start caressing my neck.

"Jesus, that was better than last time. As impossible as that sounds."

This brings a giggle out of her. "Honestly, just this—*us*—is still impossible for me to wrap my head around." I nuzzle my head in her neck, breathing her in.

"Impossible? No. Unexpected? One hundred percent."

"Why not impossible?" she asks, continuing to drag her nails down my back.

"It feels right, which means it wasn't ever *not* in our cards."

She stills for a moment before continuing the drag of her nails. "I never thought it that way."

"Well, now you can," I whisper, so exhausted from sex, the day, and everything in general. My body is begging for sleep. Her body is warm and so cozy, I could knock out right here on top of her.

"After Bennett, I never thought it would be possible. That it was never in my cards. He got the happy ending and I never did." Her voice is quiet as she confesses this. I look up and she's focused on the ceiling.

"We're all allowed second chances."

Her eyes become glossy and she takes a deep breath. "Yeah, we are." She pauses for a moment, swallows, then continues. "I am."

"Yes, *you* fucking are. Don't ever doubt it, Katherine."

She finally tilts her head to look at me. Despite the tears begging to fall, she keeps her composure. "You're right. Just took me some time to figure that out."

"I'll be here to remind you," I reassure her. "You're not destined to stay stuck. You can dream bigger and get what you want. There's no holding back, Darlin'. And just like you told me, your past shouldn't define you and never will. It's up to you to take the steps to change your course."

She sniffles and takes a deeper breath before exhaling. "I think I already am," she admits.

And shit, I can say the same for myself. To be honest, life seemed to be turning around very quickly the last two weeks and it's obvious what it might be. *Who* it might be.

"That damn mistletoe really did its job, huh?" I suddenly say.

She laughs and turns her body so we're cuddling, staring at each other. "That damn mistletoe caught me so off guard and yet here we are."

"Here we are," I repeat, my heart feeling like it's grown three times its size just staring at Katherine Pearson.

Here we damn are.

SIXTEEN

KATHERINE

LANCE ISN'T in the bed when I wake up and my heart rate skyrockets. Fuck, did he really slip out in the middle of the night? I look around the room for any notes he might have left, but there aren't any. There's a thump and the kitten is crawling toward me.

"Hi, Snowy," I say, grabbing her and placing her on top of my stomach. She begins to make biscuits on the blanket on top of me and I scratch behind her ears.

I feel almost deflated, like someone picked up a needle and popped me like a balloon. The only thing right now keeping me from breaking down is Snowflake once she starts meowing and hopping off me. She must be hungry and I don't have any cat food. I do vaguely remember having some canned tuna in my pantry.

As I get up and ready, I make sure to double check the room, even the bathroom, for any notes.

I wasn't about to ignore this. If he was going to leave after *amazing* sex, then he needs to be an adult about it and tell me. I huff out a breath and Snowflake meows, defending me.

"Let's get you some food." I beckon Snowflake and she runs as quickly as she can, slipping on the hardwood. Once I have her a plate prepared, she's happily munching and I go to check the living room and sigh. No sign of Lance.

That's when the front door opens and I whip around, ready to fight whoever is breaking in. I pick up the nearest object, a red ornament, and hold it up high.

Lance walks through the front door, grunting and sliding something big.

"Lance?" I call out. He's buried underneath the damn tree that he got me last night. I drop the ornament and run to help him.

"Fuck, this is heavier than I thought. Old man wasn't joking at the tree stand that it's a two person job."

"You should've knocked or said something! I honestly thought—" He groans and I push away my concern for the time being to help drag it inside. The floor is starting to fill with loose pine needles with each movement, but we finally make it to the corner where I planned to put the tree.

"Is there a stand or something for it?" I ask, looking around.

"On your porch. I can hold this upright if you're quick." Lance grunts and I run to the porch, grab the stand, and return to him; the air outside is brisk and I'm shivering from it. I place it on the floor and then we both hoist the tree a few inches before placing it in the holder. I'll have to get a tree skirt later.

We brush our hands off before standing back and observing our work.

"Thanks, again, for the tree," I tell him, smiling and feeling giddy like a kid again. I can't wait to put up ornaments and lights. Even though it's Christmas Eve, I'm still excited to have a tree and decorated house. I'm definitely one of those people that keep decorations up until the end of February. If it's still snowing in Tennessee by that time, then my decorations will stay, thank you very much.

Since a lot of us tend to celebrate Christmas events in Alpine on this day, and then spend our actual Christmas Day relaxing, watching movies, and being with loved ones, it makes me even more excited to have everything put up for tomorrow. Maybe Morgan and Peyton can visit and we can watch *How The Grinch Stole Christmas* while baking cookies.

With the brisk weather this morning, it's making me wonder if we'll start to get snow soon. I haven't had a white Christmas in ages.

"Sorry about this morning, I wanted to slip out to bring this inside," he confessed.

I wrap my hands around my arms, still trying to warm up and he gets close to me before wrapping his arms around me in a bear hug. He's toasty and I lean into him, breathing him in. I stare down at his cowboy boots before looking up at him.

"I thought you wouldn't come back."

His lips press tightly before he leans in and kisses me. "I think you know me better than that, Katherine."

It's true, it's just the little voice inside my head that was trying to take over this morning. "I know, it's a learning process for me to understand that not everyone will leave me behind."

"Well, I'm here now," is all he says, and I nod, reveling in that.

"I think this is starting to be my favorite Christmas yet."

He laughs. "Just you wait, I have something for you. It's in my car."

"Perfect," I tell him. "You go get that and I'll make us some coffee before we hunker down to decorate this tree."

"Deal," he responds before we break off and he runs outside.

The coffee is poured into two Christmas mugs and I leave out some sugar and cream for him to make his own and by the time he's back, he's holding a green bag. He thrusts it forward before he settles on a chair and starts making his coffee the way he likes it.

I'm excited and start digging into the bag, tossing the tissue paper in every direction. That's when I pull out the softest knitted sweater.

"What?" I exclaim, holding it up and seeing a cute little cat with various mistletoes around it. It's a little oversized, but it's so warm. I look at Lance and he's smiling bright before taking a sip of his coffee. "You made this?"

"No!" He shakes his head. "My mom did. I hope that's okay."

"Wait, your mom?" I scrunch my brows in confusion.

"Yeah. I mentioned how I found Snowflake and she was already knitting a sweater. She just didn't know who it might be for. Once she showed me the finished product, I asked her if I could take it and give it to someone special."

My heart warms at the thought. He's so selfless and he wanted *me* to have his mother's knitted talent.

"Lance, I don't know what to say."

"Well, you can wear it to the vineyard party."

I smile, cheeks burning. "I'm *so* going to wear this to the party. I think it'll be cute with a skirt and some tights. I can already picture the outfit!"

"Atta girl," he says before beckoning me over and I gladly close the distance. He sweeps me up so easily onto his lap and I wrap one hand around his neck while the other still clutches onto the sweater. I can see Snowflake running around the kitchen from the corner of my eye.

"So," I breathe, and Lance looks at me, his blue eyes seemingly even bluer than I remember, "are we going to the party together then?"

He sucks in a breath. "Oh, I don't know. That seems like it would draw a lot of attention. Especially with you in that sweater? You know the gossip in this town spreads like wildfire and they're going to talk about this." He points to the sweater.

"Oh, hush!" I swat at his chest, the sweater almost falling with the movement but he catches it in time.

"I'd like to go to the party with you, Katherine," he finally states, and now my whole body feels hot.

"Perfect." He pulls me in close and kisses my forehead before kissing me. It's not long before Snowflake's meows break our kissing and we both laugh.

"Time to decorate the tree!" I say, hopping off his lap.

Lance grabs our coffee mugs and follows me to the living room, even making sure to turn on the TV and play some Christmas music with a fake fire going on the screen.

LANCE PARKS his truck at the Vineyard parking lot and turns toward me, unbuckling his seatbelt.

"I have one more present for you, do you want it now or tomorrow?"

I turn my body toward him. "Another present? This sweater was enough! That damn tree was enough, Lance."

I'm wearing the cute Christmas sweater with a brown suede skirt, black tights, and brown Uggs. There's been a shift in the weather ever since we started heading out toward the vineyard, and the sky is starting to encase the town with more clouds than normal.

He leans over my side of the truck and opens the glove compartment, pulling out an envelope. "I know, but those weren't really your presents. This is."

The envelope drops in my lap and I take it, opening it. There are two pieces of paper folded inside and I pull the first out, unfolding it. It's a receipt to a cabin.

"What's this?"

"A weekend getaway to the mountains, if you'd like."

My eyes widen. "Really?"

He nods. "I reached out to Izzy, I hope that's fine. She told me about a cabin to rent that gives one of the most incredible views of the Smoky Mountains from its balcony. I looked up some cool hiking spots and then fun things to do in the small town there for us."

He's about to go on, but I interrupt him by leaning over and kissing him. "This is perfect. You didn't have to, yet you did. It's really the best Christmas ever, Lance."

There's a slight blush creeping up his neck and face. "You really like it? I was terrified that you'd think it was too soon. But I know I just want to spend more time with you and since we both want to start adventuring out of Alpine, this seemed like the best idea. I told you how I wanted to start my list after Christmas, so this would be the perfect first trip."

"And it is. You are," I declare.

"You are too," he remarks. "Now, look at the other piece of paper."

I put the receipt back in the envelope to make sure I don't lose it and then pull out the other. Unfolding it, I read its contents briefly and then look at Lance. "It's the bucket list."

"*Our* bucket list. I added a few things you'd like to maybe do and then some I'd like to do."

I look at the list again and see what he means.

Smoky Mountains weekend trip
New York to visit Peyton and Morgan
Colorado to visit Lance's brother
Nashville to visit Lainey

The list goes on for a few more locations and my eyes go misty, but I try my best to not let the tears fall. I've never had anyone be this intentional with a gift. But here's Lance with *several* that have so much meaning.

That's when it happens, so fast that we almost miss it. Until it happens again.

We both whip our heads to the windshield and more and more come.

Snowflakes. Matter of fact, *snow*. On Christmas Eve, of all days.

Like a Christmas miracle.

Lance grabs my hand and squeezes it before I squeeze it back.

"You ready?" he asks, gesturing toward the vineyard. There are more people starting to enter the lot to park while snow is falling everywhere now; I really hope it stays and sticks to the ground. And judging by the way the sky starts to darken, I know we're in for a very white Christmas this year.

I nod, ready to take on anything with him even if it's this holiday party.

"Let's go," I tell him.

THE END

COMING SOON BY GRACE ELENA

Katherine and Lance will reappear in future novels. Keep reading to see what's next in the Tennessee Roots Universe.

P.S: Yes, Lainey will get her own book. Take a peek at the title for the Nashville series!

ALPINE RIDGE SERIES

Between the Vines
Camilla and Bennett's Book

*Cowboy Under the Mistletoe**
*A Very Moore Christmas***

Sweet like Brittle
Birdy and Steve's Book
(Sweets Shop Owner x Mechanic)

Untitled
(Redacted x Redacted)

Untitled
(Redacted x Redacted)

*Holiday Novella (Book 1.5)
**Holiday Special (Bonus Short Story)

MASON POINTE SERIES

Melting Paletas
(Paleta Shop Owner x Firefighter)

Untitled
Adeline Monroe's Book
(Bull Rider x Country Singer)

Untitled
(Dive Bar Owner x Redacted)

Untitled
(Sheriff x Redacted)

NASHVILLE SERIES

Under Neon Stars
Lainey's Book
(Country Singer/Songwriter x Songwriter)

Untitled
(Baseball Player x Redacted)

Untitled
(Paleta Shop Owner x Redacted)

STANDALONES COMING SOON

These books are separate from Grace Elena's **Tennessee Roots Universe**. In no specific release order.

Vowed
An Accidental Marriage in Vegas Romantic Comedy

Untitled
A Military Marriage of Convenience Romance

Untitled
A Small Town Cowboy Brother's Nanny Romance

Untitled
A Modern Day Witch Romantic Comedy

THANK YOU

I always thought the more books I write, the easier this section gets. I have so many people to thank that sometimes it never feels like it's enough. But here's a start:

Thank you to all my readers who are so patient with me. I haven't published under Grace Elena for quite a while (it's been over a year since BTV was published) and I'm in awe of how many have been so excited for this novella. I can't express my gratitude to the readers who immediately jumped to support this idea when I didn't even know it would be published. You guys are my rock.

Thank you to my beta readers Andrea, Bianca, Hilary, Jenni, Jess, Kaity, Lindsey, Lizzie, Meaghan, and Tiffany. Your feedback was so helpful and it made me so happy to know how much you enjoyed the rough draft of this novella.

To my editor Ellie, thank you so so much for everything you've done with this novella. I was on a tight deadline (that I made myself) and you magically had an opening. Call it fate. I am so thankful to have had this novella edited by you and I hope we can continue to work together in the future.

To my PA, Lizzie, thank you for continuing to be so vital to this author career and always being there when new ideas pop up. You have a knack for marketing and everything under the sun for PA duties and I hope you are able to continue to thrive in this role. You were meant for it.

To my friends, new and old, thank you for always being there and holding my hand through it all. I am in awe of my village and can't believe there are such supportive people in my life for a career that is often looked down upon by others.

To my brothers, thank you for supporting me states away and showing me that distance doesn't always mean distant. You guys show up for me in your own ways. Love you both.

To my mom, thank you for everything you do. For being so proud of me every single day. For shouting to the rooftops, and the sky, that your daughter is an author. For always allowing me to come back into your arms when life takes its toll on me. A mother's love is so rare and I am so proud to call you mine. *Te amo, mamá.*

Lastly, to my dad, thank you for being the best dad a girl could ask for. I tried to dedicate my debut novel to my past partner for being the blueprint to the love I want so badly in my life, but honestly it doesn't hold a candle to your love. Not just for me, but for mom. You've shown me in my 28 years of life that even through hardships, physical ailments, and anything else that life throws at you that if you continue to show up with love that you can get through anything.

It took me a while to realize that my high standards for a partner are because of how *spoiled* I have been with a father like you. I want someone who treats me just like my dad does, but even then I don't think it would ever compare. He'd have to try his damn hardest to beat that.

There were some scary things that happened toward the end of this year and it really got me thinking of how thankful I am for you. No one can replace you. No one can bring sunshine to others lives like you do. And no one can be as hardworking as you. We are so much alike, sometimes it's scary to realize the older I get (therapy helps).

But I guess that's why you're my favorite person. From always volunteering to be the parent on field trips, being the one to show me country music with John Denver on repeat, allowing me to fail and being there to pick me right back up, and letting me chase my dreams in Tennessee when I could've easily stayed in Chicago and went to DePaul...I am who I am because of you. I love you.

"Perhaps love is like a resting place, a shelter from the storm. It exists to give you comfort, it is there to keep you warm, and in those times of trouble when you are most alone, the memory of love will bring you home."

Take Me Home: An Autobiography
John Denver

ABOUT THE AUTHOR

Grace Elena is a Mexican American author who loves to write slow burn romances with strong Latinx leads. She's been writing since she could remember and even dabbled in some songwriting during her college years. When Grace isn't writing, she's spending time with her cat in Nashville, Tennessee.

If you like more forbidden romances, Grace writes under another pen name G. Elena. Check out those books for more spice and more fun!

Visit her website at graceelenaauthor.com or you can keep up with her on Instagram @graceelenaauthor.

If you'd like to have more insight to her books before anyone else, join her Private Facebook Group "Grace Elena's Vineyard."

KEEP READING FOR BETWEEN THE VINES

first two chapters

ONE

CAMILLA

Is this where the road turns? Or is it past the willow tree on my right?

My eyes scurry across the spattered windshield, full of small bugs and leaves from the long drive, until I meet the end of the pavement where there's a sign.

A very tiny, faded green sign. It's a small arrow pointing left where the town is. The town I practically picked out by opening the map on my phone, closing my eyes, and zooming in on a random state.

Okay, to be honest, I had the map pulled up for the southern part of the United States... I needed sun if I was going to move out of Chicago. I did not want to pick Wisconsin accidentally.

Alpine Ridge, Tennessee: 15.2 miles.

Alright, I guess I'm going left. I check my rearview mirror to make sure no cars are racing down the abandoned road behind me and make the turn. Instantly, my wheels are hit with a different road surface. Gravel and dirt.

Great. I take a deep breath, press my foot on the gas, and bring on the slow journey in my small, light-green Volkswagen beetle. Guess this is the start of my life in the country. I'll make the best of it.

My parents swore I would need to trade in my car for something more reliable for my chosen southern town, but I couldn't let her go. Eucy, short for Eucalyptus, was the first car I got when I was in college, and I would be damned to get another if she was working just fine.

As the gravel and dirt meet the wheels of my Bug, I turn up the music in the car and roll down the windows even more. All that's in front of me are pastures, barn houses, and a few water towers here and there. I had a split second of doubt that the sign wasn't showing me toward town. Maybe a teen hit it with a bat and turned it in a different direction.

I push down those thoughts, allowing myself to enjoy the view and music. My right hand rests on the wheel while my left hangs outside the window, running through the soft wind like waves.

The weather in Tennessee is nothing like Chicago. It's nearing the end of April, and I still had a jacket on when I began my drive this morning. There is sunlight scorching through the windshield, and I can already feel a tan forming on my hands that are facing the spots of sunlight streaming into the car.

I can't help but smile at the thought of summer being so close because of this weather–the lakes, boats, and even the small-town festivities that would start happening. There's supposed to be an amazing cove nearby where a ton of boats and people go during the warmer months.

Or at least that's what I read online when I googled *What to do in Alpine Ridge, Tennessee.*

As the car shakes and the music blasts, I let my mind wander into the good things to come. Even if there are struggles, I can't wait to persevere through them and come out with learned lessons.

This is something that my best friend back home, Viola,

always admired about me. She says I see good days even if there is a constant storm. I won't let anyone push down my positive personality, even if they try their hardest. I'll be damned if I let them.

By the time the tenth country song comes blasting through the car's speakers, I'm nearing the end of the gravel road and finally see some buildings that I assume are the start of the small town of Alpine Ridge. I can already tell I will need to find a car wash to get all the gravel, dust, and dirt off my car.

As I let my eyes settle into what's in front of me, I hear birds chirping nearby and *no city noise*. I let myself enjoy this silence, settling back in my seat before I press my foot slowly on the gas and enter the town's lines. Everything is greener here, brighter and warmer.

I pull up to the nearest curb in the small street, survey my surroundings, and see a sweet shop, a legal office, and a salon on one side. On the other side of the street where I parked, there's the realtor business where I have an appointment to sign papers and pick up my keys.

Next to it is a cute little boutique with ivory French doors and a redheaded woman standing in front wearing a long, baby blue sundress. Her hair cascades down her shoulders, and short bangs frame her face perfectly. I can't tell if she's a customer at the shop or the owner.

Getting out of my bug and making sure the windows are up and the doors are locked, I check the streets for any pay-to-park meters, but there are none. I keep a giggle from coming out as I mentally curse myself for thinking a small town would make locals pay for parking.

I place the car keys into my black tote and pull the straps over my shoulder. Checking the watch on my left wrist, I see I am a few minutes early. My sandals hit the sidewalk as I approach the building with *Samson Realty* on the front. The reflection from the windows let me readjust my outfit from the long drive. I settled on some jade green overalls this morning, and I don't regret it with the way the sun is beaming down on me. My mom wanted me to wear a hoodie and leggings.

As I grasp the metal handle of the door, I catch the eyes of the redhead, who is peering at me with curiosity before smiling at me and turning back to what she was doing. I attempt to smile, hoping she saw it, but I know seeing someone in town walking into the realty building is not a good sign.

After pulling the handle until the heavy glass door opens, I find myself in a bright lobby with a few white cushioned seats to the side and a glass table with a cheery receptionist. A marble counter to the right has a glass fridge fully stocked with refreshments, snacks, and business cards. I see a corkboard on the wall above the marble counter where other businesses display their cards and photos.

"Hello! How can I help you?" The receptionist's voice is angelic, and her brown eyes meet mine as I step forward and give her a big smile.

"I have an eleven a.m. appointment with Mr. Oliver Samson? I have some paperwork to do."

She nods before turning her head towards a computer screen and typing. "Yes, you're buying out the Stone Vineyard, correct?"

I nod.

"He'll be right with you; he's finishing up a meeting with an investor."

"Okay, thank you so much."

"No problem, darlin'."

I turn on my heel, settle in the cushioned white seat, and sigh, letting my body relax in the elegant chair. My car and suitcases were the only things I brought here. I would need to get furniture and more clothes for this weather.

I was told that the house came as is, so I hope there is at least a mattress on which I can put my clean sheets. My mom wouldn't let me leave for my trip until I packed a whole suitcase full of cleaning products and clean bed sheets. She even taught me how to clean a mattress in case this one is in worse shape than I'm hoping. She used to work at a hotel when she just moved to the United States, so she was adamant that I knew what to do when I got here.

This thought alone brings a drop to my stomach, making me realize that I really am here in Tennessee. I dropped practically *everything*. I don't know how I will survive living in an enormous house on fifty acres of land without my parents. We've never lived *without* each other.

"Ms. Morales?" I look up to see a well-groomed man in an all-black suit walking towards me.

I get up from the chair, close our distance, and shake hands. His dark brown hand envelopes my tan one. His grip is firm and professional.

"Thank you for meeting with me this early. I know we planned for a later time, but I was already on the road."

"Don't worry about it, ma'am. I assume you're tired from traveling, so let's start."

His voice is deep and calming, and his brown eyes are soft as he nods towards the door he just came out of. I smile at the receptionist, who gives me a small wave.

"So, I will tell you that this was a surprise when I got your email. Few people requested this place."

We're walking down a brightly lit hallway until he stops in front of a large white door and pushes the handle. The room is vast, and posters are all around the walls of land, homes, and the town. Some of them look like they were from before I was born. It makes me wonder if this is a family business and if these photos have been here for a while.

"Do people not want a vineyard?" I try to joke, but Mr. Samson turns towards me with a pained face. He motions me with his hand towards one of the black leather chairs in front of a glass desk. He takes a seat next to me instead of at the desk.

"I want to let you know something. I couldn't tell you this over the phone—"

My mind instantly goes to the worst, and I let out a shaky

breath. Of course, I drove all the way over here for plans to fall through. I knew it. No matter what I do to make things go right, something *would* jinx it.

"Hey, don't look so defeated," Mr. Samson cuts me off, and his eyes glide over my face. I can't help but notice how he's even more handsome in person. He seems to be a little older than me. Before I can think more about his appearance, he continues, "The previous owner of the vineyard moved away abruptly."

"Okay," I respond.

"Andrew and Peyton Stone lived on that land for years. Andrew sadly grew deathly ill a few years ago, and as much as they tried, he passed. They left everything as is when Peyton decided to sell the land and move with their daughter."

I nod slowly, and I can feel my chest tighten. I didn't think I'd get an ownership history lesson with a plate of heartache. There would be some tough shoes to fill.

Mr. Samson waves his hand and laughs as if trying to stop himself from getting emotional with the memory of these Stone people. "I'm not trying to get you to back out. I just want you to know what you're getting into. This town of Alpine Ridge is like a family. We stuck up for each other, and we loved the Stones. I just want you to settle in with that knowledge."

"They don't want me to tear down the vineyard and build apartments," I joke, and Mr. Samson chuckles.

"Exactly."

"I assure you, I just want to continue the tradition and find my place here. I worked at various wine stores towards the end of my college career and then at a vineyard up in Chicago for four years. They made me do some of the business side until I decided I needed a break from the city and that place."

"Well, I hope Alpine Ridge treats you well. I can already tell we'll get along," Mr. Samson says with a big grin. He gets up from the leather chair and walks over to the glass table where there are a few papers. He gestures with his fingers for me to follow.

I brush the overalls until they're no longer wrinkled and walk up towards the glass table. There's a sketch of the land on three pages. One of the vineyard, the blueprint of the house, and then a sketched map of the land. I widen my eyes and curse under my breath.

It's a lot of land and one of me. Fifty acres is bigger than I thought now that I have these visuals.

"Don't worry, I had that same face when I signed my land," Mr. Samson chuckles as he hands me a silver pen.

I look up at him, and his eyes are observing me. I give him a small smile before leaning over and signing where he's pointing at the papers.

After we're done, he hands me the three papers of sketches before going towards the back wall where there is a safe. He punches in a few numbers, and there's a green light. He opens it and rummages through it before he pulls out a keyring full of keys.

He walks back towards me and hands me the keyring. I widen my eyes again at the number of keys. There are at least five.

"Welcome to Alpine Ridge, Ms. Morales."

TWO

BENNETT

"Quit it!" I yell, waving my hands in front of me.

The rooster is standing on the henhouse, screeching at the top of its lungs. He woke me up at five a.m. and again two hours later once I fed the animals and attempted to hop back into bed.

He is going to make me go insane if he keeps up with this screeching every couple of hours. My jaw clenches at the thought of him howling into the middle of the night. My shotgun would definitely make him shut up.

I throw a few pebbled grains at him, causing him to screech at me again, his small head darting back and forth from the front of the pasture next to me. He doesn't even bother getting off the henhouse to eat the grains I threw. Pathetic.

Fuck this rooster, I think as I throw a few more pieces at him and turn my back, sighing. The sun is still beaming hard on the farm, the constant drenching of sweat making me annoyed once more. My once light gray shirt looks dark gray the longer I stay outside.

It's almost May, so we have more rainy days than sunny in Alpine Ridge, but those sunny days can get up to seventy-five degrees. It might not seem very hot, but when you're not near any shade in the middle of nowhere, the sun has nowhere else to beam besides onto you.

With it almost being dinner time, I have a few more chores to get done. Feed the horses, make sure the chickens are in their coop, and check on the cats in the barn. I could spend hours in that barn playing with those cats, more than I'd like to admit.

Once those chores are completed, I rack my brain for what's left to do before the day is gone. I have to check on the plum trees that are finally blooming and make sure Lushie, the cow, has ointment on her ankle. A few weeks ago, a snapping turtle got a good nibble at her. I was in the pasture when it happened and luckily intervened.

The vet said she's been healing well, but I need to continue to lather some ointment on her wound.

Steve Robinson, my best friend since I can remember, is coming over after he's done at the shop. He should have already been here since it was past six, but he always tends to his Harley after hours. I mean, I don't blame him. He owns the shop and can do whatever the fuck he wants.

As I make my way out of the wired gate that's wrapped around the henhouse, I cast my eyes over the pasture and onto the main road. It's barely visible, but I can see a tiny car to the right of my land drive-by. Its headlights are on even though sunset isn't here yet.

With the way it's heading, they're most likely headed out of town or towards the marina. There's nothing else past the left side of my property besides empty land that has yet to be sold. There's even more unsold land to my right—making me the only occupant on this road.

I like it that way.

I have no neighbors—well, I had the Stone family live down the road, but they left years ago. I haven't had time to check on their land in the last few weeks, but I'm sure Oliver or Steve have.

We, locals, try to take our turn checking on their land in the event Peyton and their daughter Morgan ever want to come back.

It's unlikely, but we still put in the effort for that possibility. I got used to being the only human being on Misty Creek Road. The Stone's land is about three times the size of mine.

I try not to think too much about him or his family. It was so sudden the way he got ill, but it was also a very long departure. We had time to say goodbye but didn't have time to process what was happening to one of our local families. I still keep in touch with Peyton and Morgan, but it's hard when they no longer visit. I think it's hard for Peyton to come back to a place that holds so many memories of her husband.

The rooster screams again behind me, and I blink a few times and try to recenter myself. I count to ten and then list five things I can see. It happens a lot—getting stuck in my thoughts and staying there for a while, unable to process real life and what's going on around me.

I continue walking down the torn-up grassy path that leads from the hen area to the pasture.

This land wasn't something I picked out. My parents left it to me after they passed away, knowing my sister, Riley, wouldn't take it.

Riley left as fast as she could. Once she graduated high school, she picked the furthest college she could drive to and made roots in Washington. I haven't heard from her in months.

Sometimes it's better that way, with how we left things when she moved years ago.

I lift the muddy latch off the black pasture gate and push it open, letting out a grunt as the heavy gate attempts to sway back into place. The pasture is quiet. I usually let the horses out at night, but I like to keep them up in the barn in their stalls during dinner time. I don't need to stress myself out with them in the pasture with the cows. Although I tried not to keep the horses and cows in the same pasture, they seemed not to mind. I used to have an electric fence dividing the pasture into two big ones, but I kept finding a horse or a cow on the other side.

I'm not too sure how they could either jump the electric fence or get through it. It's still a mystery, but I took down the fence, and nothing bad happened.

"Lushie!" I call out. I make my way toward a wooden picnic table near the right side of the pasture gate, where I keep a milk crate full of reins, bits, fly spray bottles, and medicine. Since the forecast said no rain this week, I've been keeping it out here for easier access.

I sigh, grab the white tube, and turn towards the rest of the pasture and see an array of cows grazing or napping.

I have ten cows, but I plan to sell two to Steve soon. He finally gave in and bought some land recently instead of staying at those snobby Westland cookie-cutter homes. They're nice but not built for Steve and his lifestyle. I could never see him in those homes, but he tried so hard to fit that mold after graduating college and opening his shop. Turns out he didn't like the marble counters and tiny yard—not to mention the crazy Homeowners Association rules in that small area.

He always asked me to move in right next door, but I'd rather get deployed again than buy a home there.

I'm content with my farm here.

"Lushie!" I call out again, and one cow turns its head lazily towards me. I raise my arm and wave the tube of ointment. She hates this time of day, but I see it as a good bonding moment for us.

"Come on, baby girl!" I shout as I walk faster. She's a bigger build than the other cows, which makes me think that's why she could get away with minor wounds from the snapping turtle.

I had a horse once get its whole shoulder bitten, and the wound was so deep that there was nothing we could do. It kept getting infected even months after treatment. We had no other option than to put him down.

Within a few more yards, I'm finally closer to Lushie, and she continues to graze as I approach her. Her brown spots are bright and almost orange. I lay my hand on her hide, and she shivers from the touch.

"Hey, it's okay," I calmly tell her. I continue to rub my hand over her and allow her to get used to the feeling of being touched. I do the same thing with my horses when I have to check on them.

I lean down towards her back left leg, assessing the wound. It's looking nice and healing extraordinarily. My free hand brings the ointments closer to my other hand, my thumb pushing the cap open, a clear ooze coming out. I lean over more and steady myself as I smear the ointment on Lushie.

Unlike the first couple of weeks I had to do this, she doesn't move. She would continue to whine and adjust her cloven hooves until I had to yell at her and attempt to hold her in place.

Now, she continues to graze the grass as I smear more ointment over the pinkish wound. I can see some hair grow again, and I smile.

"Good girl."

Lushie responds with a moo, and I grunt as I get myself back up into a standing position. I close the cap on the bottle and pat her back.

"You did good. Now you can continue to eat."

I glance around the pasture again, ensuring nothing is conspicuous on the land. Last week, there was a snake that blended well with the grass. A horse stepped on it, thankfully.

"Alright, guys. I'm headed inside. Don't party too late," I joke, turning my back on the cows who continue to nap or graze.

I suddenly remember the plum trees and make my way out of the pasture towards the back of my house. There's a strip of trees that I started growing once I got ownership of this land. There are some lemons, oranges, plums, and blueberry shrubs.

As I get closer to the trees, they seem to be doing well. I keep them a few feet away from each other so as not to cross-pollinate. I had that issue years ago when I had two apple trees. They became a hybrid of each other. Although I expected extra sweetness, they were pretty bitter. The plum trees look promising and are sprouting small plum bulbs. It will take a week or two for them to reach full size.

I grab my phone from the back pocket of my jeans and see that Steve texted me a couple of minutes ago.

STEVE

On my way. I got news for you.

ME

I just finished with Lushie. I'll leave the door open.

STEVE

You're not even going to ask what the news is??

ME

If it's something that will help this rooster shut up, then I'm all ears.

I hit send on that last text just as the rooster screeches again, and I clench my fists, almost breaking my phone.

"Fucking rooster."

I hear the engine of Steve's bike from a mile away, and it becomes louder as he gets closer to the entrance of my property. The crunch of the gravel is loud, and I can hear everything. I can pinpoint exactly where he is on the pathway towards my house. That's the downside of living in the middle of nowhere with no neighbors: I can hear every animal and any small sound if I'm not busy. At night, there are coyote screams that I've gotten used to.

It only becomes a real problem for me if I notice any of my chickens missing, and I need to watch overnight near the window facing the chicken coop. My .22 long rifle is perfect for that job, scaring the coyotes and raccoons.

Sometimes, when I'm bored and can't sleep from the noises, I'd rub some camouflage paint on my face, dress in all dark green and black attire, and find a spot on the ground near the coup.

Steve joined me once but complained that he was too 'one with nature' and ended up ruining the shot I had at a raccoon entering the coup.

I was perfectly content there in my face paint and dark clothing. It reminded me of my years out in Colombia. The thrill and excitement of that time in my life was something I've always tried to chase again. It's hard when those years are supposed to be behind me. I'm just left with nightmares and panic attacks instead.

"Bennett!" Steve yells as his engine shuts off, and I open the screen door. He positions his bike on the kickstand and then jogs over. His white shirt is greasy, and his face still has some stains from the shop. His blonde hair flops in the front as he walks across the yard.

"Hey, man," I say as he gets closer and nudges me with his shoulder before pushing me inside. I roll my eyes and turn to pat him on the back as he makes himself at home—literally. He waltzes into the hallway, past the living room and guest room, until he's in the kitchen. I trail quickly behind him. It's a small house, but it has what I need. The second floor has a few more rooms and an attic for storage.

"I wasn't too sure what we wanted for dinner, so I was planning to get takeout," I respond.

Steve leans back on the kitchen counter. It's a pretty outdated kitchen that I've yet to renovate. It's next up on my list.

He crosses his arms and sighs. "It's okay. I got caught up cleaning my bike and talking with Oliver."

I nod and step towards the fridge, opening the heavy door and pulling out two beer bottles. I hand one to Steve as he nods, and we both pop off the bottle tops with ease.

"How's Harley? And how's Oliver?"

Steve shrugs. "She's good. Just needed a quick oil change. I've been using her too much–I'm changing her oil almost every month."

"Jesus, Steve. How far are you taking her?"

Steve chuckles before taking another sip of his beer. "Apparently too far. You know me, driving wherever the fuck the road goes. I have no destination, and Harley knows it."

"And Oliver?" I remind him.

Steve looks at me and then smiles before answering. "Right. He called me around four, and he threw a curveball at me when we were about to hang up. He said someone bought out the Stone's land."

There's silence in the room, and I grip the bottle tighter in my palm.

"You're kidding," I respond, attempting to calm myself before Steve asks what's wrong with me.

Steve shrugs again. "He won't give me any details. I told him he's just being a pussy and that he's not a doctor with some HIPAA shit to abide by."

I let out a laugh and shook my head. "I'm pretty sure he's still allowed to keep the privacy of new landowners. I wonder if it's some investor wanting to build million-dollar homes."

"I mean, you live near the marina. It wouldn't be such a bad idea."

"It would be horrible," I disagree.

"For you."

"Exactly."

Steve and I stare at each other before busting out in laughter.

"You're never gonna let someone live next to you, huh, buddy?"

"Not a chance unless it was you," I respond, taking a big chug.

"Yeah, I kind of fucked up on that part. I wanted land near my shop. Sue me," Steve responds with another shrug.

I place the bottle on the counter near the fridge and cross my arms. "Well, where do you want me to order takeout from?"

"I was actually going to suggest that we go out."

"Like a date?" I ask with a raise of my eyebrows.

Steve chuckles and then waves his hand. "I'm flattered, really,

Bennett. But your anger issues would make me move to Timbuktu."

I laugh, and Steve does, too. Really, we could be brothers with how often we get on each other's nerves, yet we can continue to be friends.

"Why not go to Nicky's?"

"That dingy old bar you hate?"

"Yes, that one." I roll my eyes and lean my head back in exasperation.

"Alright. But if you get into another bar fight, then I'm dragging you out."

"I can handle myself," I chuckle. Steve looks at me with one raised brow and then barks out a laugh, holding his chest with his right hand.

"Sure, sure. They have mouth-watering fried pickle spears."

"And wings. And beer," I add, and Steve nods.

I follow him out near the entrance of my place and grab the keyring off the hook near the front door before locking the door from the inside. We head towards the side of the house where there's some pavement for me to park my vehicles.

Steve heads towards the truck that's on the left of the bike.

"Shotgun!" Steve yells as he opens the door and gets into the shotgun seat.

"You're hilarious, man," I say with a straight face before Steve lets out a howl.

"Alright, let's head to your favorite bar," Steve yells as he rolls down his window and leans his head out, ready for the wind to catch his hair like a dog.

I shake my head, push the key into the ignition, and turn it— the truck rumbling to life.

www.ingramcontent.com/pod-product-compliance
Lightning Source LLC
Chambersburg PA
CBHW011856300726
48970CB00009B/2818